Edgar Wallace was born illegitim
adopted by George Freeman, a por
eleven, Wallace sold newspapers at Ludgate Circus and on leaving
school took a job with a printer. He enlisted in the Royal West Kent
Regiment, later transferring to the Medical Staff Corps, and was sent
to South Africa. In 1898 he published a collection of poems called
The Mission that Failed, left the army and became a correspondent
for Reuters.

Wallace became the South African war correspondent for *The
Daily Mail*. His articles were later published as *Unofficial Dispatches* and
his outspokenness infuriated Kitchener, who banned him as a war
correspondent until the First World War. He edited the *Rand Daily
Mail*, but gambled disastrously on the South African Stock Market,
returning to England to report on crimes and hanging trials. He
became editor of *The Evening News*, then in 1905 founded the Tallis
Press, publishing *Smithy*, a collection of soldier stories, and *Four Just
Men*. At various times he worked on *The Standard*, *The Star*, *The Week-
End Racing Supplement* and *The Story Journal*.

In 1917 he became a Special Constable at Lincoln's Inn and also
a special interrogator for the War Office. His first marriage to Ivy
Caldecott, daughter of a missionary, had ended in divorce and he
married his much younger secretary, Violet King.

The Daily Mail sent Wallace to investigate atrocities in the Belgian
Congo, a trip that provided material for his *Sanders of the River* books.
In 1923 he became Chairman of the Press Club and in 1931 stood as
a Liberal candidate at Blackpool. On being offered a scriptwriting
contract at RKO, Wallace went to Hollywood. He died in 1932, on
his way to work on the screenplay for *King Kong*.

More
Educated Evans

HOUSE OF
STRATUS

This edition published in 2001 by House of Stratus, an imprint of
House of Stratus Ltd, Thirsk Industrial Park, York Road, Thirsk,
North Yorkshire, YO7 3BX, UK.

www.houseofstratus.com

Typeset by House of Stratus, printed and bound by Short Run Press Limited.

A catalogue record for this book is available from the British Library
and the Library of Congress.

ISBN 1-84232-699-6

We would like to thank the Edgar Wallace Society for all the support they have given
House of Stratus. Enquiries on how to join the Edgar Wallace Society should be addressed to:
The Edgar Wallace Society, c/o Penny Wyrd, 84 Ridgefield Road, Oxford, OX4 3DA.
Email: info@edgarwallace.org Web: http://www.edgarwallace.org/

CONTENTS

THE RETURN OF THE NATIVE   1

A SOUVENIR   16

THE MAKER OF WINNERS   28

A JUDGE OF RACING   38

AN AMAZING SELECTION   49

A GOOD GALLOP   60

A HORSE OF THE SAME COLOUR   71

MIXING IT   83

THE FREAK DINNER   96

THE USER OF MEN   107

THE LADY WATCH DOG   119

THE JOURNALIST   129

THE RETURN OF THE NATIVE

It is an axiom of life that the course of true love never ran smoothly.
There were certainly snags in the current of Mr Cris Holborn's affair,
but the largest and most considerable of these was Annie Beaches'
mamma, who was stout and snacky. She snacked Mr Holborn about
his profession – she herself being a lady of property and owning the
house in Mornington Crescent; she snacked him about his
gentlemanliness; she snacked him on the question of stable odours –
she invariably held a handkerchief to her bulbous nose when he came
into her drawing-room – and she snacked him about his education.

Sometimes, in desperation, Mr Holborn snacked back. He told her
that he was one of the best known trainers of race-horses in England,
that he was 'Cris' to scores of the gentry and nobility, and that if a
farmer's son was not good enough for the daughter of a retired
publican, well, he'd like to know who was?

It may be said in passing that Mr Beaches had not only retired from
The Trade, but he had also retired from earth, and at the moment was
resting at Kensal Rise under a huge slab of Aberdeen granite, on
which was carved a tissue of falsehoods concerning his virtues as a
father and husband, and his great loss to the world.

And in a sense Cris Holborn's retort was justifiable. He was one of
the best known trainers in England and one of the cleverest. In the
language of the crude men who support the art and practice of horse-
racing, he was hot, and when his horses won, he won alone:
sometimes not even the owner of the horse was aware of the
forthcoming jubilations.

On a night in February Mrs Beaches snacked to such purpose, and was supported so effectively by her charming daughter, that things happened in Mornington Crescent. Neighbours heard the sound of shrill and angry voices, a door slammed violently, and there was the sound of breaking glass...

Peace reigned in Selbany Street Police Station. The station sergeant nodded over his book, the policeman on duty at the door yawned frequently and wondered if the clock over Disreili's, the High Class Jewellers, had stopped.

The hour was 1 a.m., and it was raining greasily as it can only rain in Somers Town. It had been a dull evening, being Thursday, when men go soberly to their homes and play draughts with their children and win – if the children have any discretion. A night when the cinemas are half empty, and the landlord of the Rose and Cabbage leant his bloated hands on the counter and severely condemned socialism to an empty saloon.

There were only three men and one perfect lady in the cells at the back of the station: Crime for the moment was unpopular.

Detective-Sergeant Arbuthnot Challoner, whom men called The Miller because he chewed straws, came in hastily out of the darkness, and hung his raincoat on a peg.

"Yes," he said sardonically in reply to the grey-haired station sergeant, "it *is* a nice night!"

The clock ticked solemnly and noisily.

"Nothing doing?"

"Nothing," said The Miller shortly. He had been standing for two hours in the rain waiting for a car thief who was expected to retrieve the car he had garaged.

At that moment, when the night seemed as barren of promises as the pages of Dr Stott's sermons, a car drew up opposite the station entrance and there sailed into the charge room Miss Ann Beaches and her ma. Miss Beaches was golden-haired and blue-eyed. She wore an evening dress of gold and crimson and a fur jacket. She had orchids at her waist and about her neck a choker of imitation pearls the size of pigeon's eggs. Her ma was more soberly arrayed in black with glittering jet ornaments.

"Is this the police court?" asked Miss Beaches with a certain ferocity.

"It is the police station," said The Miller.

Annie closed her eyes and nodded.

"That will do," she said quietly. "I wish to have a summons against Mr Cris Holborn for insulting my dear mother and breach of promise, though I wouldn't marry the dirty dog not if be went down on his bare knees to me! He's a low type and if my poor dear father had been alive he'd have bashed his face in!"

"He would indeed," murmured Mrs Beaches.

The Miller would have explained, but –

"When a lady lowers herself to be seen out with a common horse trainer," Miss Beaches went on rapidly, "when she does everything for a man as I've done, introducing him into society so to speak, and when he didn't even know what a fish knife was till me dear mother taught him, it's hard to hear your dear mother called an interfering hag."

"*Old* hag," murmured Mrs Beaches. "Don't forget the winder glass, Annie."

"I'm coming to that, ma. Also I wish to charge him with breaking two panes of glass in our front door by his violent temper. I'm going to show this man up! Him and his lords that he knows!"

"Which we don't believe," prompted Mrs Beaches.

"And the words he said about publicans is a disgrace," Annie went on, "him and his horse that's going to win at Lincoln – "

"With twenty-one pound in hand," added mother under her breath.

"With twenty-one pounds in hand?" repeated The Miller thoughtfully.

"That's what he says," said Miss Annie, "though I know nothing about horse-racing, my dear papa having brought me up very strict. Now I want to know if I can't have a summons – "

3

"Excuse me. Miss," said The Miller gently, almost benevolently, "what was the name of this horse?"

"I can't think of it for the moment," said Miss Annie, to whom the identity of the animal was much less important than the exposition of her grievances; "but if I did know I should tell that common man that always used to be hanging about Camden Town – Elevated Evans."

"Educated Evans," corrected The Miller. "He's not living here just now, but if I can do anything in the way of spreading the good news – "

"That's neither here nor there," said Miss Annie tartly. "Can I have a summons?"

And The Miller explained that summonses were never granted at a police station, and certainly never granted at one o'clock in the morning. He also expressed his doubt as to whether the offence of Mr Holborn had been as heinous as she imagined. To the best of his ability he gave her the law on the subject. It is not unlawful to refer to a future mother-in-law in terms of opprobrium, and he also explained that the word hag, whilst it might mean a vicious old lady, might also describe one who could bewitch.

"At the same time," he said sympathetically, "I feel that I would like to help you get your own back, Miss Beaches, and if you would mention the name of this horse I'd see – "

At this point the silent mother became voluble.

"It's no good your wasting your time here, dear. They can't do anything, and if they could they wouldn't. All these men stick together. The best thing to do is to see your dear father's solicitors in the morning. If I don't have the law on Cris Holborn…"

They made a noisy exeunt.

It was rather strange, as they say in Somers Town when they mean to imply coincidence, that this reference to Educated Evans should have been followed up that very morning by the appearance in court of a local larcenist who in the old days invariably traced his downfall to the fact that he was a subscriber to Educated Evans' £5 specials; for Mr Evans had been the World's Champion Prophet and Turf Adviser.

Miss Beaches had gone home with her mother, some of her ardour for vengeance a little cooled. She awoke at nine o'clock to find her mother with a letter in her hand. It had come by hand from her outrageous lover – she recognized his novel spelling.

"Ah, well, Ma!" she said: "Perhaps I was hard on him: I knew he'd send me an humble apology first thing in the morning."

"It's got to be humble." said her ma ominously. " 'Ag I may be, but old I'm not!"

"You've got to allow something for youth," said Annie, romantically, as she tore open the envelope. "The poor boy wasn't himself– "

She read the letter: it was very short.

"I'm done with you and that old nagger your ma. I'm lowering myself to associate with a lot of pub keeper's relations. Farewell. Never cross my path again. CRIS.

PS – Send back the ring I gave you *I may want it.*"

Ann didn't scream, she did not faint. She pulled on her dressing gown.

"That settles him!" she hissed.

Her ma was making savage noises. Annie ran to the door and pulled it open.

"Em–ma!" she screamed.

'The maid' – in reality a backward 16 year old who came daily – flew up the stairs.

"Go and find that tipping man you was – were talking about yesterday – go and bring him here at once!"

She returned, rolling up the sleeves of her dressing gown pugilistically.

"Nagger…!" moaned her ma.

"Goin' to make thousands of pounds, is he!" said Annie fiendishly. "I mustn't tell anybody, mustn't I? I'll show him… Digger Boy! That's the name of the horse, Ma! Digger Boy – I'll Digger Boy him."

She said other things – such as may be pardonable in a lady under the sad circumstances.

In the meantime Emma was searching Camden Town for a local prophet who was not without honour in his own district.

A day or two later Camden Town was startled by the most stupendous item of intelligence that had been dropped in years.

Educated Evans was back!

The news ran like a prairie fire from the Goods Yard to the Holloway Road – from Great College Street to the Nag's Head. Men heard and halted their pint mugs between counter and lip and said "Go *on!*" Some confessed that they thought he was dead; others corrected this impression regretfully. Down at the White Hart an old man stirred and glanced uneasily at the door. Miss Pluter, the new barmaid at the Stag and Crown – she who wore 'Jenifer' in diamonds across her blouse – expressed a desire to see the man about whom she had heard so much, and a dozen knights and squires of the saloon bar offered eagerly to fetch Evans the very next night.

Mr Evans had returned to the scenes of his vicissitudes and triumphs! He had once gone through the card at Kempton one remarkable day and had made two, three, five, ten thousand pounds according to the source of report. He had retired; he was an owner of houses; he had an estate in the country and occasionally wrote to former clients on notepaper headed Hillsden Hall, Pilberry Road, Hollingbourne, Kent, and that in printed characters.

It was believed that he had a servant of his own and was so rich that he wore a clean collar every day of his life. Further, it was alleged by one who had visited him that he had his dinner at the hour when most respectable people have finished their tea and are having a sluice in the kitchen preparatory to a visit to the cinema. This story, however, was not credited.

Nor did the news of his return find general acceptance. Camden Town had been an uneducated place since Mr Evans drove away in a taxi smoking a Masa cigar ("all the fragrance of Havana for 1/6.") waving his hand graciously from the window. Many a man who could not afford a mouthpiece regretted his going, for Evans was as good as a lawyer, and had composed many an address calculated to move the stoniest-hearted magistrate. It was Evans who got Bill Barrett off a lagging by a defence – read by Bill in the dock – showing that he had suffered from loss of memory and sleep-walking since a child. Bill certainly boggled some of the words – his pronunciation of somnambulism was wonderful to hear – but there were tears in his eyes as he read things about himself that he had never known till that moment.

In the days of his activities Educated Evans had had one faithful retainer. His name was Samuel Toggs, and it was generally believed that he had been so christened in the dim and glorious ages when hansom cabs were a novelty and malefactors were publicly executed before Horsemonger Lane Gaol. He was called 'Old Sam,' partly because Sam was his name and partly because of his many years. His occupation in life, in those days, was the support of the White Hart, a noble hostelry. He supported this palace of sin by keeping his back against it from 10 a.m. to chucking-out time. A strange, burly old gentleman, with tender feet and an opalescent beard that might have been white with care, he wore, summer and winter, two overcoats and a pair of black woollen mittens, a woollen scarf and a bowler hat that he had found in the roadway after a fight one Christmas Day.

Mr Evans had been a force in Camden Town, being an educated man and one learned in the ways of thoroughbred race-horses. So, if you believed him, no horse won unless he had received Mr Evans' express permission to do so, and that in writing. Sometimes he gave them permission and they didn't win but, as he said, horses are not machines. He asked his clients – for he supplied information for a trifle to all who acted honourable – to remember that he gave Braxted (What a beauty! What a beauty) at 20-1. He made a lot of money and retired to the country: what was more natural than that, when he lost a lot of money, he should come back to Camden Town?

It is strange that, as Educated Evans had journeyed towards the metropolis, he should think kindly, almost tenderly, of Old Sam. That beer-soddened ancient was in a sense a protégé of Evans'. Though from morning until night he propped up the walls of the White Hart, standing with his back firmly fixed to the wall, and refusing to be enticed away by any save the barman, he had made an exception in the case of Mr Evans, for whom he ran errands, hobbled about with messages to clients, and sometimes collected money on behalf of his patrons. Old Sam had touched his cap to the educated man and had once called him "sir," but this was on the night that Sam had paid for his own drink twice.

It was not until two mornings after his return that stress of business permitted the educated man to look up his old acquaintances, and it was by a pure accident that the first of these should be The Miller – a lover of racing and no bad friend to Evans.

Mr Challoner was standing opposite the Cobden statue, doing nothing, when his absent gaze rested on a man who was walking up Bayham Street. He was not tall, he was not broad. He was to an extent well-dressed. In one corner of his mouth was a large cigar. and if his cap and plaid trousers did not accord with his black jacket, he had the air of a nobleman.

The Miller's jaw dropped as the man came nearer, for he recognized instantly the World's Premier Prophet and Turf Adviser.

"Well, well!" said The Miller, when the first greetings were over. "So you're back, and Camden Town has one more mug."

"It's all very well for you to go passing personal remarks," said Educated Evans, with a touch of asperity in his voice, "but what's the good of locking the stable door after the horse has ate his wild oats, I ask you, Mr Challoner?"

Sergeant Challoner did not take offence at the brusqueness, even rudeness, of the reply, but continued to nibble his straw reflectively, his grave eyes fixed upon the Prophet.

"You had a fortune," he said slowly. "You won it by being clever enough not to back your own tips, and by reducing yourself to a condition of beastly intoxication before you went racing. When you handed up your money and told the bookmakers what horse was going to win, you happened to speak the truth – *in vino veritas*."

"I know Veritas – he's a two-year-old in Perse's stable – but Vino is an animal I don't remember."

"Having accumulated this wealth, you took your ill-gotten gains, purchased a farm, and not only committed the unspeakable folly of owning racehorses, but added the general lunacy of attempting to train them."

Educated Evans shook his head sorrowfully.

"It was the feeding that done it," he said. "Was I to know that horses didn't eat bones and birdseed? Is there a book published on the subject? Did Mr Gilpings when he wrote his highly clarsical articles in the weekly newspapers, mention anything about feeding animals? Anyway," he added hopefully, "I'll get it all back over the Lincoln. There's a horse in that race that hasn't been tryin' for four years. There's a big stable commission, and he's *loose!* This horse could hop home on his fetlocks. I'm sending it out on my Five-Pound Owner's Special Wire, so don't put it about, Miller."

The detective sighed.

"Camden Town has been a dull and truthful place without you." be said. "What's the name of this horse?"

"Otono," said Educated Evans. "I've got a thousand pounds to twenty about it from Issy Isaacsheim."

The Miller rubbed his nose thoughtfully.

"He was scratched this morning," he said gently, and Evans made a clucking noise with his mouth.

"Thank Gawd I didn't back him!" he said, and did not even attempt to excuse his perjury. "With that animal out of the way, it's a stone certainty for Cold Meat. That horse has been specially kep' for this race. I've had it from the boy who does him."

"When you get anything good, you might come and see me," said The Miller, preparing to depart. "Cold Meat's been put out to grass. I thought you might have seen it in the papers yesterday."

He waited, and then:

"How's Old Sam?" asked Evans.

The Miller looked at him.

"Haven't you heard?" he asked, in a hushed whisper.

"Not dead?" asked Evans, preparing to be shocked.

"No," said the Miller, and then: "There's no room for you here, Evans – you've lost the art of tipping losers."

Mr Evans shrugged his shoulders.

"It's a historic fac'," he said, "that once you're a bricklayer you're always a bricklayer. It's in your blood. Look at Napoleon Bonaparte, the well-known French officer. When he was took away an' imprisoned on the Isle of Dogs did he sit down an' moan? No, Mr Challoner, he sees a spider comin' down from the ceilin' an' he says 'Turn again, Napoleon,' an' sure enough he did."

"What?" asked the dazed Miller.

"Turn," said Evans, "an' I've turned. When I read in the so-called sporting press the ad. of this feller an' that feller – actually boastin' about the 7-4 winners they've give, I remember Braxted – 20-1. What a beauty! an' Eton Boy, 100-8. What a beauty! an' such like high-class predictions an' prophecies, an' I says to myself, 'Evans,' I says, 'don't let them daylight robbers have all the loot to theirselves – 'op in and help yourself.' "

Mr Evans gave a hitch to his shepherd plaid trousers, lit again his tousled cigar and wiped his newly-grown moustache on the back of his hand.

"Did Camden Town hang out its flags when you came back?" asked The Miller.

"Sarcasm don't mean nothing to me," said Evans; "it passes me by like Cardinal Rishloo, the highly respected clergyman said, like water on a duck's back in one yerhole and out of the other yerhole."

"I seem to have heard that ancient one before," said The Miller. "What are you going to do?"

Evans studied the busy prospect of High Street before he answered.

"I'm gettin' together my army of touts," he said. "I've appointed me Newmarket an' Lambourn men – an' to all clients new an' old I say 'Fear Nothing!' "

"And what do they say?" asked the interested Miller.

Evans coughed.

"They ain't had time to reply yet," he said. "I only sent out yesterday to a few clients – about three thousand."

"Liar," said The Miller softly, and Evans smiled as though he knew better. "Seen anything of young Harry Leafer – he used to be a client of yours?"

The question was carelessly put but Evans shot a suspicious glance at him. For the whisper had gone round, and it had reached him, that young Harry had disappeared suddenly and urgently only that morning. It was even said that he had gone to Brighton or some other foreign part.

"I don't know nothing about young Harry," he said, hurt. "Can't you get it out of your head that I'm a nose, Mr Challoner?"

"Nose is vulgar – say unofficial detective," murmured The Miller, and made preparations to go.

"Look up Old Sam: he'll be tickled to death to see you," he said at parting.

Educated Evans sniffed.

"The likes of him look *me* up," he said. "He knows where to find me."

There are few keener pleasures than the happy sense of anticipation which is enjoyed by the wanderer returned to his native home. He pictures the enthusiasm which the news of his return will bring; he sees in his mind's eye men crossing the road to greet him, or the shy children he left behind, now radiant and beautiful young women, advancing timidly to hold his hand, and gazing with awe upon one who has ventured abroad. Educated Evans had not been abroad, but Hollingbourne is a very long way from Camden Town.

He saw no recognizable shy maidens, High Street being notoriously deficient in this quantity. Nor did anybody run across the road, in imminent peril of being run over, to grasp him warmly by the hand. The landlord of the Red Lion gave him a curt nod and did not seem to be aware of the fact that he had been away at all. An acquaintance of other days certainly joined him at the bar at his invitation, but Evans realized that he would join anybody who uttered that magic password to conviviality, "Wotshors?"

"How's Old Sam?" asked Mr Evans.

His guest for the moment coughed and looked uneasy.

"Oh, he's all right," he said, and changed the subject.

"I'm opening my new office this week," said Evans carelessly.

His acquaintance coughed again.

"I hope you'll give some winners," he said unpromisingly.

"Braxted," murmured Evans. "People have got a short memory."

"Personally I was at school when Braxted won," said the other with a certain significance.

At the Old Albany Arms, Evans found two clients of other days, and broke it to them that he was back in business. They seemed uncomfortable. When he asked after Old Sam they were embarrassed.

Was the aged man ill? wondered Evans as he strolled forth into the High Street, and there came upon him the spirit of philanthropy and loving-kindness. Old Sam used to live in a house up a very narrow passage which was called locally Little Hell, though there were many people who thought that the adjective hardly described the character of the place.

Evans called. Old Sam's landlady was out. Her slatternly granddaughter told him that Old Sam was living in Great College Street. Mr Evans was shocked. Great College Street is a thoroughfare more or less devoted to the plutocrat.

He sought out the address: a highly respectable and classy one. There was a lawn in front of the house and white curtains at the window, and the girl who answered the door piped that Mr Toggs was out, and would Mr Evans come into his sitting-room and wait?

Educated Evans went out into the street, a little dazed. Had Old Sam come into money? He was to learn

He wended his way to his newly recovered flat in Bayham Mews. He referred to it as a flat, though in truth it was one room over a garage, and he was very lucky to get back his old quarters. Fortune had come to him, as The Miller had said, and he had started forth upon a hectic career as owner and trainer, freely backing his own horses, in consequence of which he had returned to Bayham Mews with ten pounds, one pair of plaid trousers, a gold-plated razor and a few inconsiderable articles of property which he had salvaged from the wreckage of his estate.

Evans had work to do. He had acquired for a song a patent duplicator. A child could work it. There was in fact a picture in the advertisement of a pretty little girl turning out thousands of copies in an hour and smiling the while, as though at the ridiculous ease with which handbills, accounts and announcements of all kinds – to quote the literature which accompanied the picture – might be copied. Evans would like to have met that child. He guessed she was a weight-lifter in her spare moments.

It was easy enough to write your announcement on the special paper. Then you fixed the wax paper on the machine, inked a roller and turned a handle. At first nothing happened. Then a violet oblong, covered with all the available ink, came out.

Evans preferred a rubber stamp or, alternatively, the services of a young lady in Great College Street, who did that kind of work at a reasonable price and with great rapidity and could, moreover, use a typewriter.

Nevertheless, he determined on one more attempt with the patent duplicator. So working, he heard the slow thump of feet on the wooden step that led to his door, and presently the door itself opened, revealing the bulbous face of an aged man. It was Old Sam. But Old Sam in a black suit – Old Sam in a bowler!

"Hullo, Evans," said Sam huskily, and Evans nearly dropped.

"Hullo, Evans!" And this from a man who was, so to speak, a slave! He blinked into the room suspiciously.

"Hullo, Evans," he said again.

The educated man waved his hand haughtily.

"Push off – I've got nothing to give away," he said.

Such a rebuff would have reduced a sensitive man to tears of mortification. Old Sam scratched himself thoughtfully.

"I gotta tip for Digger Boy first day at Lincoln," he said, and Evans gasped at the insolence. Even in his delirium he realized that he'd never heard of such a horse as Digger Boy. But imagine the feelings of Michelangelo in receipt of a letter from a Florentine Correspondence School headed 'Let us Show You How to Paint –

13

Send No Money!' or Shakespeare being chided at rehearsal by a small-part lady for splitting his infinitives.

"A what!" asked Evans, scarcely believing his ears.

"Got it from the young lady who knows the trainer," wheezed Old Sam, stroking his variegated beard. "What a beauty, what a beauty! Help yourself!"

The room spun round. This...this common loafer, this holder-open of taxi doors...this embeered and senile servant to the pot...actually employing terms which were sacred to Mr Evans' exclusive profession!

"Wait a minute – a young lady gave you this...horse? Why?"

Old Sam came farther into view. He was resplendent. A cable chain of gold was stretched across his portliness. He wore patent leather shoes.

"She sent for me," he said hoarsely, "me havin' a reputation – she sent for me!"

Evans held on to a chair for support. Had the great revolution arrived? Had the masses destroyed the intelligentsia of the country and assumed control of affairs? Were the lower orders on top and the aristocracy of brains destroyed?

" 'Ere, what's the game?" said Evans, a little breathlessly.

Sam looked uneasy for a moment.

"When you went away I took up this tippin' business an' I've done well," he said. "Can't read myself, but got a boy to look through the papers, and if I liked the name I give it – 'aven't you heard of Old Sam's Specials?"

Evans was not dreaming.

"Old Sam's Specials?" he repeated hollowly. "What did you sell 'em for?"

Mr Hoggs shuffled his feet in embarrassment.

"Sixpence," he said, and Educated Evans nearly fainted

"Sixpence!"

He looked round for something to throw at the visitor, but there was only the patent duplicator, and even a child could not have thrown that... Sam was half-way down the stairs before Evans could bring his numbed brain to work. He rushed to the landing and looked down into the face of the plagiarist.

"...Robbin' my brains, you perishin' old swiper..." he yelled.

"Digger Boy...'ad 'im from 'eadquarters!" bellowed Sam. "An' don't go pinchin' any of my customers!"

Evans put on his hat and went out to make enquiries. It was true. Almost every little newsagent in Camden Town sold Old Sam's Specials.

"I admit they're different to yours," said one agent, and added: "They win."

It was night time when the real tragedy came home to him. He called at the White Hart, expecting to see Old Sam supporting the wall and to pass him by in disdain. He saw The Miller talking to a policeman near the saloon entrance, but Old Sam was in the private bar. Evans heard him as he opened the door.

"I gotta horse for Lincoln that can't lose...this horse could fall down an' get up an' win. Lady sent for me specially to tell me. She says, 'Are you the well-known Educated man?' I says, 'Yes, miss – I'm known as Educated Toggs...' "

Evans flung open the door with a savage howl and dashed in.

It was fortunate that The Miller saw and gripped him in time and dragged him out: most unfortunate for Sam that he followed in a valiant mood: a crowning calamity that he should mistake the uniformed policeman with whom The Miller had been talking for his old patron, and should assault him with a beer mug.

They carried Old Sam to the station in an ambulance, and the next morning an unsympathetic magistrate sent him down for three weeks.

"I hated putting the old man away," said The Miller. "Anyway, Evans, the coast is clear for you now your rival has gone."

"Rival!" sneered Evans. "That pie-can! Why, he don't know a horse from a step-ladder. I wish he'd been out when I started my season! I'm sendin' out a horse that couldn't lose if he was scratched."

"What horse is this?" asked The Miller.

"Digger Boy – help yourself – and don't forget I've got a mouth!" said Mr Evans.

A SOUVENIR

Through his uncurtained window Mr Evans could see the young lady in grey. She occupied the room immediately opposite his own and on the other side of the mews. Her uncle was a musher and drove a taxi which he, and his brother George had purchased on the never-never system. Her aunt was genteel and wore glasses. They lived in a large suite of rooms which extended over two garages, in one of which the cab was cleaned: it never stayed there for any appreciable time. The uncle drove it by day, and the other uncle, whose name was George, by night, or *vice versa*. The taxi never complained about this perpetual motion because it was inarticulate.

Evans was not interested in the cab, or the uncle, who always seemed to have boils on his neck, or Uncle George, who was a thin, acidulated man who talked to himself all the time. Nor did he look twice at the aunt. But the niece in grey, with her black hair and her way of putting her hand on her hip, this young woman was, and had been since she first nodded to him brightly and said "Morning," an object of profound speculation and delight. Sometimes she nursed a baby prettily. He discovered in subsequent conversations that it was her sister's.

Mr Evans was not old. On the other hand, he was not young. And anyway, scholars have no age: they are youthful or ancient according to the measure of their erudition.

"I'll bet she wonders who I am," said Mr Evans with a quiet, sad smile. "Few people know me outside of the profession. I'll bet she says, 'I wonder who that lonely man is: he looks as if he's had a lot of trouble – an' what an interestin' face he's got, mother or auntie, as the case may be!' "

Thus Evans communed with himself before the mirror, not knowing at that time the exact relationship of the lady with the driver of cabs.

One evening he leaned over the balustrade of the landing outside his door. She came out, looked and nodded.

"Evening," she said. "It's a nice evening."

"Not so good as Palermo in the South of France, or dear old India," said Evans. "Give me Egyp' for nice evenin's an' a half-hour's row down the Nile Canal."

She looked at him awe-stricken, red lips parted, violet eyes wide opened.

"Have you been there?" she asked.

"Lots of times," said Evans carelessly; "*and* China, which is the most highly populized country in the world. That's where we get china from an' Chinese lanterns."

She leaned over her landing too. There was twelve feet of space between them. Down below a dazed neighbour stopped to listen.

"It must be wonderful going abroad."

Evans shrugged so violently that one of his brace buttons came off and fell with a musical tinkle on the cobble-stones below.

"You get used to it if you're a racehorse owner," he said. "I've won the Calcutta Cup once but I gave away the ticket to a footman at my club – couldn't be bothered. The Melbourne Cup – that's a wonderful race! Down in Orstralia."

She drew a long, sighing breath, her eyes were bright. He had, he saw, assumed a new interest in her eyes. The glow of it made his woollen vest feel prickly.

"Fancy...you own racehorses! Do they ever win?"

Evans smiled tiredly.

"Now and again. I don't like winnin' too often. The other members of the Jockey Club get that jealous there's no holdin' 'em."

"But how mean!"

Evans started to shrug again but remembered in time. Down below in the mews, the neighbour collapsed against the wall.

"You can't please everybody," said Educated Evans. "Even Queen Elizabeth couldn't do that – that's why she got her napp – her head cut off by B – Mary the celebrated Queen of Scotch. That led to the Diet of Worms an' the rise an' fall of the far-famed Oliver Cromwell, fourteen hundred and seven'y-six," he added.

She was stricken speechless for a moment, and Educated Evans proceeded.

"That brings us to the question of Astronomy. Very few people know that the eclipse of the sun is caused by the earth in its revolutions comin' between the moon an' the sun, thus causin' many ignorant people to think that the whole thing's wrong, when as a matter of fact it's an act of nature."

He was now speaking fluently, swinging his hat with the same easy carelessness as a sailor swings the lead. And when he dropped the hat into a puddle immediately below him, he just smiled. He was that careless.

"Take the law," he said. "There's a good many people don't understand the law. Many a time I've stood up in court and said to the other lawyers – "

"Are you a lawyer too!"

Below, the neighbour tried to say that Mr Evans was less of a lawyer than a something liar, but his lips would not frame the words.

"Bit of everything," said Mr Evans modestly. "Scientific – take sidlitz powders – "

The beautiful girl in grey was spared the need Her aunt appeared in the open doorway a mass of undigested knitting in her hands, and called her in.

"Come in, Clara, do!"

"Yes, auntie," said the girl meekly.

"What on earth do you want to talk to that old man for?" demanded the aunt, too audibly: the rest was undistinguishable.

Evans sneered at her. Old! What a nerve! Still, he had impressed her: he could see that. He went down the wooden steps, retrieved his hat and his button, and returned to the privacy of his 'den' to dry the one and sew the other. She knew him now for what he was. An educated man. She was probably talking to her aunt about it at that moment, chiding her parent for her uncharity.

"No, auntie, you are wrong. I won't allow you to say that. He is *not* old – and what is age? One loves a man's mind; his breadth – his education."

That's what he imagined her saying. What she actually said was: "Who *is* that funny old geezer, aunt?"

"God knows," said her aunt, a pious woman. "I think he's something to do with dogs."

But Clara Develle was honestly and sincerely interested in Educated Evans and wondered about him. For example, she often wondered if he was right in his head. And she wondered who gave him his plaid trousers, and she wondered if he was a burglar, but decided that he was too tender on his feet for that nippy profession. And as her wonderment grew, there came to her a realization that there really were possibilities about the educated man.

"Never mind about *him*," said her aunt sharply, when she approached the subject. "Your uncle Alf says things can't go on as they're going. You've got to find something to do. He can't keep you in idleness, because we're poor people, and if we wasn't we wouldn't."

Clara said nothing.

"Your uncle's a man of the world – so is your uncle George," her aunt went on. "There's some things we don't know and don't *want* to know. Certain things have been remarked, but the least said soonest mended. Only it seems *funny!*"

Her niece was evidently in agreement with these cryptic sentiments, hints and innuendoes, for she sighed sadly. Evans did not see her again that night, but he did notice, as he had noticed before, a young man going up the steps after dark.

Dark suspicions gathered in Evans' mind. Could this young man be a Fellow? Was he a Chap? The thing was preposterous...such a child...the aunt would never allow it. Not if she was a Good Woman...

Occasionally The Miller drifted down Bayham Mews. Generally it was a matter of duty which brought him to this place of silence, but sometimes he mounted the wooden steps that led to the habitation of Educated Evans, in search of social relaxation – for even a detective-sergeant has a human side to his character.

On this chilly night in March, The Miller came up the steps and knocked at the door.

"Hullo, Mr Challoner!" said Educated Evans graciously. "Kindly step inside and take the chair."

"Have you got a meeting, Evans?" asked The Miller good-humouredly.

"No – but I've only got one chair," said Evans.

He wore his overcoat, for the night was cold and the fire was weak. The Miller glanced at the table, covered with a litter of paper.

"Just writing to a few of my clients," said Evans. rubbing his long nose. "They don't deserve it, but I've got to do it – Cold Feet for the Hurst Park Hurdle. He's been kept special for it. Not a yard at Lingfield – but this time his head's loose."

"Old Sam says – " began The Miller, but the look of pain, reproach, contempt and acid amusement in Evans' face cancelled his communique.

"I'm sorry I mentioned your rival," said The Miller.

The pain in Mr Evans' face grew more acute.

If The Miller had any reason for his call he did not state it. Evans was almost glad to see him go. Great was his fortune when later, slipping out to get a quick one, he met the grey girl at the end of the mews. He had an impression that she had just seen somebody off – a brief blurred glimpse of a figure vanishing in the darkness. Should he speak to her or pass with a stately bow?

"Good evening, Miss – ?"

She knew his name.

"Miss Develle," she said. "Just been seeing a friend off," she went on. "Not exactly a friend, but a gentleman who is always running after me."

"What a cheek!" said Evans hotly. "I never heard such a thing in my life. It's preposterous!"

They lingered awhile. Her eyes shone hotly out of the dark; the dusk of night was in her hair. Evans grew agitated. It was within five minutes of closing time.

"I'd like to have a chat with you, Mr Evans," she said earnestly. "You're such a Man of the World, or Gentleman of the World as one might say. I'll be going to the Rialto cinema at seven tomorrow night. Please don't mention it to auntie."

She was gone before he realized; her black hair and violet eyes were swallowed in the void. Educated Evans reeled to the nearest house of refreshment and drank heavily, for him.

They met in the ornate vestibule of the Rialto and slipped into the dark interior.

"...Yes, my aunt. My father married beneath him – he was a Colonel in the army...that little baby's my sister Molly's... Oh, I'm so glad to have a chat with you, Mr Evans! I'm in such trouble. I must get some kind of work – I really must. It's hateful depending on relations or even relatives..."

She told him of her struggles; of the weary round she went from aunt to aunt –

"There's a cashier wanted at Lammer's. That's my work...if only I knew somebody who knew somebody else who knew Mr Lammer."

Honestly she was not aware that Mr Lammer was an acquaintance of his. When he explained that he had only to crook his finger for Mr Lammer to skip like an intoxicated lamb, she thought he was showing off. The most she had expected of her new-found friend was an unusual angle which would help her.

When the lights went up he saw that she was a little older than he had thought. This pleased him. He paid for a light fish supper out of his last five shillings and went to bed full of noble resolves.

Mr Evans, of Sansovino House, Bayham Mews, was not without influence. There were people in Camden Town who never heard his name mentioned without employing the most regrettable expressions to describe The World's Premier Racing Prophet and Turf

Adviser; but there were others who through thick and thin were loyalty personified.

Mr Lammer, the High-Class Ladies' Outfitter, for example, never ceased to sound the praises of one who, at a critical moment in his history, when every other man who came into his office carried a writ of summons in his inside left-hand pocket, had imparted to Mr Lammer the exclusive information that Braxted could fall down, have a fit and *then* win the Steward's Cup.

The distracted Mr Lammer had in his possession at the time the sum of five hundred pounds, which he had put aside for the rainy day when he would be obliged – in the language of Camden Town – to do a bolt. This sum, withheld from his creditors, he invested on Braxted at 20/1. And Braxted won. Twenty times £500 is exactly £10,000, and with this sum Mr Lammer paid his debts, extended his premises and entered upon a newer and brighter life.

He was not a cultured man, being one of those who admitted responsibility for his own success, and he admired beyond words the erudition of his humble friend.

"Certainly, Mr Evans," he said, as the educated man sat on the edge of a chair in his office and made his request, "I'll do anything I can for you. I've given up backin' 'orses, but if you're ever short of a few pound, step in and ask for what you want. You say that this young lady is All Right?"

Evans drew a long breath.

"She's the daughter of a colonel in the Army," he explained fervently, "and a perfect lady: Owin' to a bank failure the family's ruined. She's like the celebrated Dick Whittin'ton an' don't know the way to turn. And she reminds me of the well-known an' highly respected wife of Julius Caesar, the far-famed Italian – she's above the position."

So it was arranged that Clara Develle should go into Lammer's store as junior cashier at a reasonable salary, and Evans purred his way back to Bayham Mews, where the young aristocrat was in residence, and waited for the friendly dark to tell her the good news.

"I must say it's awfully good of you, Mr Evans," she said rapidly – she was rather a quick talker. "What a bit of luck for me that I met you as I did! I'm sure my poor pa would have died with shame if he knew I was going into business – as a matter of fact he died from eppoplexity during the air-raids, him being a General and naturally brave."

Educated Evans scarcely noticed her parent's promotion.

"Has that feller been worrying you again?" he asked with a sub-tone of ferocity.

On the previous night they had discussed the furtive young man who came and went in the dark. Evans had recognized him.

"Mr Erman? Oh dear, no." she protested. "I'd never dream of looking twice at him. Saucy monkey if ever there was one."

"I saw him talking to you in the mews tonight – " began Evans.

"Merely passing the time of day. One has to be civil in my position. I mean to say, you've got to be polite if you're a lady," she said breathlessly.

Evans, the loyallest of men, felt she should know the worst.

"He's a crook, a hook, and a twister," said Evans. "He's done time for burglary and he owes me two pun'ten over Charley's Mount, what I put him on to. Remember, miss, if there's any trouble, I'm around!"

She said she would remember: She said this rather vaguely, as though she were thinking of something else.

"You've been simply marvellous to me," said the general's daughter with a sigh, "and when I get working I'm going to give you a little souvenir."

"A bit of ribbon," said Educated Evans sentimentally, "a glove – anything to remind me of you – nothing expensive."

Things were not going well with Evans. He might have paraphrased Mr Browning and said, 'Never the chance and the girl and the money all together.'

A week later Educated Evans watched the stream of life passing along Hampstead Road, and mused a little sorrowfully on the unattainable value of things. Every bus that flew by was worth thousands of pounds; not a cyclist plodded across the field of his vision that was not supported by a couple of pounds' worth of old iron and rubber.

The landlord of his suite in Bayham Mews had that morning demanded – with a certain significant reference to the number of people who were begging and praying for the accommodation usurped by Mr Evans – that the four weeks' arrears of rent should be paid by twelve noon on the following day, failing which –

Detective-Sergeant Challoner stood by his side in as earnest a contemplation of the pageant of life. A keen wind blew down High Street, though the sun shone overhead in a blue and white sky: it was spring. Near the White Hart, the red-nosed Lolly Marks stood behind a barrow banked high with daffodils and narcissi – the placards bore the magic slogan 'Lincolnshire Favourite Coughing' – the vernal equinox had swung to Camden Town.

"If people would act honourable," said Evans, "this would be a grand world to live in. As William Shakespeare, the well-known and highly popular poet, says, 'What a game it is!' and he was right."

"Broke?" asked The Miller, with a certain hard sympathy.

Yet he did not look broke. Mr Evans for once was dressed up to his position. His moustache was trimmed, his collar was clean, and only an expert could see where he had scissored the frayed edges. A ready-made tie was embellished by a jewel that might have been a ruby worth a couple of thousand pounds, but probably wasn't.

"To pieces," said Educated Evans, and shrugged his hock-bottle shoulders. "When you re'lize that I sent out the winner of the Newbury Hurdle to three thousan' nine hundred and forty clients, and that all I had back for my trouble was twelve bob and a slush ten-shillin' note that I nearly got copped for passin', you understand why men like the celebrated Sir Francis Columbus went an' lived in America."

"Why don't you see Lammer – he's a pal of yours?"

Evans screwed up his face in contempt.

"I never touch a client," he said, and spoke the amazing truth.

"Why are you waiting here?" asked The Miller after a long silence. "Looking for anybody? By the way, you haven't seen Nosey Erman about, have you?"

"No, I haven't," said Evans. "That feller's less than the dust to me, to use a well-known expression."

"I wonder why he's turned up in Camden Town?" The Miller mused. "He's got some game on, I'll bet."

Well Mr Evans knew the game of the wanderer. He had returned to filch the heart of an innocent girl – the sharp eyes of the educated man had detected the amorous Nosey. His exposure was accomplished.

The Miller pulled at his long nose, and then:

"Come round to my place this afternoon and I'll let you have a pound," he said as he prepared to go. "But don't come if you can tap anybody else."

Between gratitude and sardonic mirth at the prospect of tapping anybody, Evans was slightly incoherent.

Long after The Miller had gone he waited, and presently his vigil was rewarded. A slim, neatly dressed girl walked quickly up Bayham Street and turned towards the High Street. In an instant Educated Evans was flying across the road, and at the sound of his voice the girl turned with a smile.

"Why, Mr Evans," she said, "I thought you were at Cheltenham!"

"My car broke down," said Mr Evans mendaciously. "The carburretter keeps on back-firing: for two pins I'd send it back to old Rolls and give him a bit of me mind!"

He fell in by her side, and for two minutes fifty-five seconds and a few fifths he trod on air, and his heart sang songs.

Just short of Lammer's Corner she stopped and held out her hand with a sigh.

"You are lucky, Mr Evans," she said enviously. "It must be wonderful to be your own master: to go where you like and how you like. I wish I had a lot of money."

Evans wished the same thing as fervently, but he did not say so.

She sighed.

"I wish I knew what was going to win that big race at Cheltenham," she said.

"Benny's Hope," replied Evans promptly. "I've had it from the owner, who's a personal friend of mine. That horse could fall down, get up, turn round to see what was going to be last, and then win."

"Benny's Hope," she said thoughtfully, and then: "I've got that souvenir for you, Mr Evans," she said. "You wouldn't think that I was fast if I brought it round to your flat one night, would you?"

And before he realized it, she had disappeared through the ornamental portals of Lammer's.

Evans walked thoughtfully back to his apartment, planning matrimony.

Educated Evans got out of bed and slipped on his dressing-gown, which was also his overcoat, an extra blanket, and on occasions a raincoat. The hour was seven in the morning; outside in the dark mews rain was falling steadily.

It was not an hour at which one might expect the most enthusiastic of clients would call on the World's Champion. In truth, of late, Evans had found his erstwhile clientele somewhat sceptical of his information even when he sought them out.

He turned on the light and opened the door. There was nobody in sight, and then he heard a sound and, stooping, lifted the long basket that stood on the landing and carried it into the room.

"Good Gawd!" said Evans.

He heard the wail before he opened the lid and saw the solemn eyes staring up from the interior of the basket.

"Good Gawd!" said Evans again.

He picked up the baby and laid it on the bed, and with a flutter of eyelids the tiny mortal went instantly into a sound sleep.

Evans examined the basket. It bore the label of a local fishmonger and smelt strongly of the sea. The World's Champion ran his fingers through his hair and strove to recover his composure. And then he heard a heavy step on the stairs, and the door opened to reveal a figure in a raincoat.

"Hullo, Mr Challoner – come in."

The straw between The Miller's teeth was sodden with rain and, as he stood in the room near the door, tiny rivulets of water dripped to the floor.

Without any preliminary:

"Do you know Mrs Erman — a pasty-faced girl with goggly eyes?"

"I don't — " began Evans.

"You got her a job at Lammer's," said The Miller sharply. "I knew she was staying here with her aunt and I came down to make sure the other night, but I never dreamt she'd plant herself on you. She was hanging round here for something, but I couldn't guess what it was."

Evans was pale, his mouth wide open.

"Wha's — wha's happened?" he croaked, and The Miller laughed unpleasantly.

"Tonight they cleared Lammer's safe and made a getaway. We'll be able to pick them up because she's got a baby."

Educated Evans opened his mouth again and tried to speak, blinked impotently and tried again.

"Miss Deville…"

"Mrs Erman," corrected The Miller, and his eyes fell on the little slumberer. "Yours?" he asked, and Educated Evans shook his head, speechless.

The Miller walked across the room and examined the child. He saw what Evans in his agitation had failed to see. A card tied to the baby's wrist by a piece of pink ribbon, and the card was inscribed:

"A little sooveneer."

Mrs Erman was good at figures, but her spelling left much to be desired.

THE MAKER OF WINNERS

The Miller would have passed the crowd at the corner of College Street, only the voice that emerged from the centre of the throng had a familiar ring, and he edged his way into the press with no great difficulty, for certain of the audience recognized Detective-Sergeant Challoner and were passionately desirous that the recognition should not be mutual.

Round and round a cleared space in the middle of the crowd walked a man who was jockey from the waist up. The colours were familiar to The Miller. He had seen them on the winners of the Oaks and he had seen them at Ascot; there, too, he had seen the great owner of the colours but he had not heard that She had engaged Educated Evans as first jockey to Her stables.

The tipster had a bundle of cards in one hand, a riding whip in the other; his jockey cap was a little too big for him, and the peak flopped down over his nose, and all that The Miller could see was a fringe of ragged moustache, the tip of a stubby nose and an unshaven chin…

"…And let me tell you people who know me far and wide, that a man of my education wouldn't go lowerin' hisself to appear in public like the famous Lady Gawdiva who rode through the streets of London with nothin' on to settle a bet, if it wasn't that I can't letcher miss the most unbeatable certainty that ever looked through a bridle. Did I give yer Salmon Trout? Did I beg an' implore yer to back Charley's Mount – did I go down on my knees to yer and say 'Whatever y'do, don't leave out Twelve Pointer for the Cambridge – did I tell you what his twelve points was…?"

The Miller waited through another quarter of an hour's eloquence; waited till Mr Evans had stripped his royal livery and resumed his coat. And then:

"I'm surprised to hear you telling the tale, Evans." Mr Evans shrugged his narrow shoulders.

"It's common, I admit – but I got to work up my connections, Mr Challoner. Competition's done it. Old Sam got my best customers. You wouldn't think that old pub-lizard could compete with a man like me. Why, I could talk him blind, Mr Challoner. Where's his education? Could he put a letter together like me? Could he get a job like I got – a hundred pound job with lashin's of money besides? No! That old Sam is a low, uneducated pub-prop! But I got him. He's for Lapwing to win the Newbury Cup an' the horse don't run. I've had it from the boy that does him. Ice Box is a certainty – tried twenty-one pound better than Blue Nose. He'll come home alone."

The Miller walked on until they came to the corner of Stibbington Street.

"I don't fancy Ice Box," he said then.

Mr Evans smiled.

"Could you fancy Twelve Pointer with six stun three? Could you fancy Pharos, the property of the celebrated Sir Derby, with no weight at all – that's Ice Box at 7-5!"

Again The Miller was thoughtful.

"I saw you with a swell in Euston Road this afternoon – friend of yours?"

Educated Evans looked important, coughed knowledgably and patently avoided the topic.

"He's an acquaintance – good night, Mr Challoner."

"Hold hard: who is this lad you were with?" asked The Miller. "Got an idea I know him."

"He's a doctor," said Educated Evans briefly. "Doctor Walling – a client."

He seemed disinclined for further discussion. The Miller watched him turning back towards Bayham Street, his colours under his arm, using his whip as a walking stick, and then of a sudden the officer of

29

the law forgot that there was such a person in the world as Educated Evans. For, glancing idly up at the dark facia of a house, he saw the figure of a man walk carefully along a parapet and disappear into a top window.

It was a large house and respectable. It was owned by a Mr Opes, a builder, who lived on the premises and had his workshops in what had once been his back garden.

The Miller crossed the road and presently a uniformed constable appeared. There was a brief consultation and the policeman went off to telephone for a few reserves.

Waiting until he had returned, the sergeant went up to the door and knocked; it was opened by a young girl who told him that nobody was home but her: the rest of the family was at the cinema. After he had explained who he was, he went upstairs and found, hidden in a cupboard, William Henry Smith, by trade a painter, by inclination a small-time burglar.

"It's a cop – I'll go quiet," said the philosophic William in plain English. "I rumbled you as soon as I took a screw through the winder. When I got my lamps on you I knew you was a busy. What'll I get – a laggin'?"

"Hope for the best," said The Miller, as he snapped handcuffs on the man – William sometimes changed his mind about going quietly.

As they walked to the station:

"I have to work for *my* livin'," said William Henry Smith bitterly. "I'm not like this here Educated Evans, that can go tellin' the tale an' the police not so much as clout him!"

One of the standing grievances of the criminal classes is the immunity of the non-criminal classes.

"What has Evans done to you?" asked The Miller, who was a tireless seeker after knowledge.

William Henry thought hard and could find no offence in the Educated Man – at least no offence that he could put into words at that moment.

"He's unlucky," he said. "It's well known all over Camden Town that if you have anything to do with Educated Evans you'll have bad luck. An' why I did a bust at that so-and-so house, when I've got a hundred pound job to do for a gent, I don't know," he added in despair. "When I come out of my house to have a stroll round I'd got no more idea of bustin' that house than I had of flyin' – I must be gettin' childish. But the fact is, Miller, I can't resist paripits. If I see a paripit runnin' round a house I've got to get up to it…"

He expatiated on the lure of parapets and threw in a remark or two about the temptation of pantry windows, and The Miller listened with great forbearance

"What was this hundred pound job you were going to do?" he asked during a pause in Mr Smith's homily.

But William Henry Smith was no squeaker.

"You said you were going to do a hundred pound job for a gentleman," said The Miller patiently. "What's the good of being silly? – I'm your best friend – "

But William Henry was deep in his gloomy thoughts.

"And there was a hundred pound job waiting for me," he repeated moodily. "A hundred pound sweet. No risk, and, in a manner of speaking, quite lawful. But the moment I knew Educated Evans was in it I ought to have run away from London, I ought indeed, Miller."

"Was he in it?" asked The Miller, as they turned into a street where the blue lamp of the station house gleamed mournfully.

"He was and he wasn't," was the cryptic reply. "He was, and yet he didn't know he was, if you understand me rightly? He's unlucky, that feller. Tipster! Why he couldn't tip a load of dirt into a shell-hole, that feller!"

William Henry had once served in the Army and his illustrations were occasionally of a military character.

When The Miller had seen his guest safely housed, and had furnished the station sergeant with a number of uncomplimentary particulars about William Henry and his past and hopeless future, he strolled home to his rooms in Great College Street, a very thoughtful man.

Educated Evans had spoken about a hundred pounds – William Henry Smith, painter, had also spoken of a hundred pounds. Was it a coincidence...?

There was at this time a celebrated racehorse named Bonny Lad. He was trained in the north and, for some extraordinary reason, he was a good horse. Everybody knows that good horses are not trained in the north. If Ormonde had been sent to a stable in Yorkshire he would have automatically become a selling plater. He would have looked round, taken a screw at the pitheads and chimneys, listened bewildered to one of the stable boys saying "Tha knows lad an' all," and would have immediately developed boils, strangles and infantile rickets. But Bonny Lad was a good horse. Even Newmarket which, according to the touts, is entirely populated by horses that could win the Derby in a bad year, admitted that Bonny Lad was a good horse and that, if he'd only been trained in Newmarket, he would have been an aeroplane.

He was favourite for the City and Suburban. That is to say, he was favourite with everybody except the bookmakers, who had laid him at all prices from 50/1 to 9/4. With them, he was no more favourite than measles in a girls' school.

As Mr Evans walked home to Sansovino House, his educated brain was occupied by thoughts of Bonny Lad, that wonderful horse; and it is a remarkable tribute to his self-control that, though the name had trembled on the very tip of his tongue, he had made no reference to this animal of quality.

Unconscious of the doubt that he had raised in the minds of the constabulary, he reached Sansovino House, which was the same room over a garage in Bayham Mews, unlocked the door, locked it again and turned on the light. Then he pulled up the ruins of a mat to keep the room airtight and began to put on evening dress. Which meant that after a sluice in a pint and a half of water, he changed into a pair of check trousers, put on a nearly clean collar, an Ascot tie – embellished with a large golden pin in the shape of a horseshoe – rubbed his shoes with a towel to raise a polish and taking down a pair of yellow wash-leather gloves from the line, fitted one with some difficulty upon his left hand, for they had shrunk in the process; after finding his walking-stick, which was under the bed, he turned off the light, unlocked the door and went forth, a model of sartorial sportiness.

A bus took him to the Oxford Street end of Tottenham Court Road, alive at this hour with throngs of the idle rich who had just been turned out of the cinemas. Passing through Soho Square, he came to a small restaurant, into which he turned. It was at the moment inhabited by a stout French lady in a dirty apron and a well-dressed man who sat at one of the tables drinking coffee. The man turned his head as Evans appeared and nodded him to a chair opposite.

"Good evening, Doctor," said Educated Evans languidly, as he handed his stick to the waiter, who handed it back to him. "Sorry I'm so late. But a couple of members of the Jockey Club called at my digs, and I couldn't get rid of 'em. They didn't half rap about the way the turf's going from bad to worse. One of 'em – Lord X: I won't tell you his name because he wouldn't like it – said to me: 'Evans, speaking as a man of education and knowledge – ' "

"Yes, yes," said the other testily. "Sit down. What'll you take? It's too late for a drink."

"Coffee," said Evans indifferently. "I've been drinking champagne all the night till I'm sick of the sight of a tumbler. As I was saying – "

"I was expecting another gentleman to come tonight – a friend of mine," said the doctor.

He was a thin-faced man with eyes that never kept still.

"But I will tell you before he comes what I want you to do. Do you know Wilmer's in King's Cross?"

"The overnight stables?"

"That is the place," said the doctor. "You told me you were willing to earn a hundred."

Evans nodded dumbly. He was willing to earn ten shillings at that moment.

"Now I have told you before, and I'll tell you again, the strength of the situation," said the shifty-eyed man, sucking at the stub of an unlighted cigar. "I'm one of the connections of Bonny Lad."

Again Mr Evans nodded, this time almost humbly. The very thought that he was hobnobbing with 'connections' was overpowering.

"Bonny Lad is arriving from the north tonight, and goes on to Epsom tomorrow," said the doctor, slowly and emphatically. "He has had a tiring journey – you know what horses are."

Mr Evans nodded slowly.

"As a owner and trainer," said the World's Best Tipster, "I understand 'em inside and outside, up and down, this way and that way, so to speak. As the celebrated George III said to the well-known Duke of Wellington, the highly renowned officer in the Army – "

"Never mind about the Duke of Wellington," said the doctor, who was disinclined at the moment to listen to any other voice than his own. "The point is that the owner doesn't want this horse" – he looked round and lowered his voice – "doped!" he hissed.

Educated Evans bit his lip and looked profound.

"But he's got to be doped or he won't win," the doctor went on. "The owner's a personal friend of mine, but I've got to look after him for his own good, if you understand me?"

Educated Evans did not understand.

"Here's the stuff," said the doctor, put his hand in his pocket and took out what looked like a tiny syrup tin. He prised up the sunken lid with a coin and displayed a brown treacly mass.

"A friend of mine will get the stable open, and all you've got to do is to get into the box, put your finger in that and let him lick it."

"Suppose be bites me?" said Evans, a cold shiver running down his back.

"Bite you!" said the other contemptuously. "You understand horses, don't you? Horses don't bite, they suck!"

"But they've got teeth," said the obstinate Evans. "I've seen 'em!"

"They never use them," said the veterinary authority. "Are you game?"

Evans was rather white by now. He coughed, looked helplessly up at the fly-blown ceiling.

"I suppose it's all right," he said uneasily. "I mean there's nothing wrong in it?"

"Should I – me a doctor of medicine and all – ask you to do anything that wasn't right?" demanded the reproachful doctor.

But Evans was not happy.

"How about getting into the stable?"

"He'll be taken to Wilmers the moment he arrives tomorrow." The doctor spoke with great rapidity. "The boys will go away to get a cup of coffee, and they'll lock the stable door. A friend of mine's going to open it – he'd have done the whole job, only he doesn't understand horses."

The doctor might have added that he himself would have done the whole job but his ignorance of the thoroughbred racehorse was almost as colossal as William Henry Smith's.

Educated Evans took the treacle pot, put on the lid slowly and dropped it into his pocket.

"What time is this other fellow coming?" he asked faintly.

That was exactly the question the doctor was asking himself; for he knew nothing about the unhappy ending to William Henry's stroll.

"I don't know," he said. "Meet me here at seven tomorrow."

The future for Evans was brighter than he dared confess. None, seeing the man commonly, indeed vulgarly, declaiming to a circle of incredulous punters, would have imagined that fortune had again tapped timidly on his front door.

Mr Evans smiled to himself as he clumped up the wooden stairs that led to the very door on which the fairy fingers of fortune had danced. What a triumph would be his when it came out that Educated Evans *was in with the owners!*

Old Sam…! Educated Evans grinned diabolically at the thought of his rival's discomfiture. That beer-burdened snake in the grass!

He blew on the end of his big key, inserted it in the lock and tried to turn it. But it was already turned: he had, in fact, forgotten to lock the door when he went out, and it was unfastened. He pushed open the door and stood paralysed with horror and indignation.

The light was on and there was a man in the room. An ancient man with a prismatic beard. He sat in a chair, his hands clasped on his waistcoat, his mouth open, his eyes closed.

Two a.m.! Mr Evans almost choked. Possibly he made appropriate noises. Old Sam opened one eye and waved a feeble hand.

"Come in… Evansh! Take a sheat…was yours?"

Evans strode into the room, his eyes glaring.

"Outside!" he hissed. " 'Op it, you ale-eatin' perisher! You are not satisfied, you uneducated old 'ound, with takin' the bread out of my mouth, but you come a-trespassin' in my house!"

Old Sam surveyed him glassily.

" 'Tain't a house, it's an aylorft," he said, and for a moment Educated Evans thought he was talking a foreign language.

The man was intoxicated. Evans shuddered at the pollution brought upon Sansovino House. And not only was he intoxicated, but he was truculently so and, surveying him, a doubt crept into Mr Evans' mind. He was old but muscular, and under the stimulus of strong drink old men have done terrible things. Educated Evans coughed, and his tone grew more conciliatory.

"You can't stay here, Sam," he said mildly. "I've got to get to bed."

Old Sam stared at him blankly.

"I'm staying here," he said with great deliberation, "till tomorrer. I got pinched over you, and you went and give away a stable secret what I got from the boy that done him. Tomorrer, you uneducated man" – Evans gasped and turned even paler – "I'm sendin' out a tip that'll knock you silly, and I'm stayin' here to see that you don't get ahead of me."

"But, Sam," said the agitated Evans, in an even more friendly tone, "you can't stay here, old man. I've got one of my clients coming up to see me here tomorrow."

"Ha!" said Old Sam. "Your client! Walker the fishmonger. He owes! I've come for an explanation."

He found the word rather difficult to say, but eventually said it.

"When I lay in the cold prison cell – at my time of life too – I thought I'd come out and cut your throat – give us something to eat. I'm starving."

Educated Evans was being ordered about in his own house.

"My dear old Sammy," he said, "as the celebrated Michael Angelo said to the well-known Lewdcreature Burgia, it can't be done."

And to demonstrate the absurdity of the whole situation, Evans took off his coat, hung it on a peg, as though, whatever happened, he was going to bed.

"Want to fight, do you!" roared Old Sam, and staggering to his unsteady feet reached for the first missile which came to his hand, which was Mr Evans' small but hard poker.

No horse that Educated Evans ever tipped moved faster than the World's Champion Prophet and Turf Adviser.

The Miller, strolling towards High Street, saw a shivering man in his shirt sleeves standing at the end of the mews.

"…Half an hour ago," explained Evans tremulously. "Come into my house and threatened to murder me! After all I've done for him! The four ales I've stood him! The perishin' old beer-biter!"

"Come along with me," said The Miller authoritatively. "We'll deal with this Trojan. What's this great tip of his for tomorrow?"

"He didn't tell me," said Evans, with some asperity. "And what's more, if he did I wouldn't take the slightest notice of it."

They mounted the steps together. The light was still on when Evans opened the door, and Old Sam was seated at the table and was talking drowsily to himself.

"…Nothing to eat in this 'ole," he mumbled, "only bread and golden surrop, and he carries *that* round in his coat pocket!"

A cut loaf was before him, and a small open tin. There was also a half-eaten slice of bread covered thickly with a brown, treacly substance.

Evans did not faint, but somehow he knew that Old Sam would not be in a position on the following day to give a tip, good, bad, or indifferent.

A JUDGE OF RACING

The honourable Mr Justice Bellfont was a very human man with a wide knowledge of human affairs. If the name of Carslake had been mentioned in his court, he would not have said, "Who is Brownie Carslake?" but would have told you the position Brownie occupied in last year's list of winning jockeys, and his lowest riding weight. If he did not tell the court this in audible tones, he would have exposed his knowledge *sotto voce*, for he had the habit of speaking his thoughts aloud.

On Saturday meetings you could see him at Kempton or Sandown, and he had even been known to journey north to witness the field of the Manchester November Handicap emerge from the fog. He had a cousin who owned horses and a nephew who trained them. He was, in the sense of experience and knowledge, the widest judge that ever sent a lad for a stretch.

He loved horses, and even in the days when he was a prosperous junior, never had more than a pound each way.

He had a notoriously tender spot for the little thief, and a hard surface for the clever financiers who came at rare intervals before him, and his terse "You will be sent to prison for seven years" had brought distress to many a family which was living in luxury on the doings that papa had extracted from poor investors.

Therefore it was, in a sense, an act of providence that Walter Holl came before him – for Walter, though a tea-leaf, was a good fellow and a well-meaning man.

In the clear grey of morning, before the shops are open and while milkmen are yet lying in their beds, Camden Town is a place of solemn splendour, and even her public-houses have an especial dignity. Save for a belated cat or so making its weary way homewards after a night spent in reckless debauchery, nothing human moved in High Street. The drone of a distant newspaper van chugging to Euston, the twitter of the birds in Bayham Street and the distant hoot of an engine at the Goods Yard, are the only sounds that break the sylvan stillness.

The Miller had spent the night profitably in conducting a raid on a snide factory just off Ossulton Street and now, at peace with mankind, he stood surveying the desert of High Street.

A figure came shuffling round a corner, saw him instantly and faded out of sight.

The Miller did not move: seemingly he had not seen the wayfarer. Presently the furtive man peered round the corner, saw his enemy standing apparently oblivious of his presence and, turning, walked back the way he had come, satisfied that justice was happily blind.

Mr Walter Holl would have found it difficult to run, for he carried in his cloth bag a large quantity of lead piping and brass taps that he had acquired in the earlier hours of the morning from an untenanted house in the Holloway Road.

He was half-way back to Great College Street when he heard the softest sound behind him, and turned to meet The Miller.

"Lord! Mr Challoner, you give me a fright! Them rubber soles of yourn ain't half quiet!"

"Been shopping?" asked The Miller pleasantly, his eyes on the bulging bag.

"Them?" Mr Holl asked innocently as he opened the bag and displayed his loot. "They belong to a friend of mine, a plumber. He's goin' up to Scotland to do a job an' he asked me to bring the bag to the station for him – gave me five bob to do it. You see, Mr Challoner, he got soused last night an' – "

"Come along and have a cup of coffee at the station," said The Miller, "and we'll talk over old times. How long ago is it since I took you for busting empty houses, Holl? Must be nearly three years."

Mr Holl fell in by his side, The Miller's hand affectionately gripping his arm.

"It's a cop," said Walter, with the philosophy of his kind. "I got these out of a house in the Holloway Road – Number 804, or maybe 408. It's hard luck on me, because I was goin' to get a packet out of Telltale in the Victoria Cup."

At the police station he was searched; before he was put into the cells he asked a special favour.

"I'd be very much obliged, Mr Challoner, if you'd ask Educated Evans to put a piece together for me so as, when I go in front of the old bubble an' squeak I've got, so to speak, a full answer?"

"Can't you afford a mouthpiece?" asked the sympathetic Miller, referring in this crude way to a gentleman learned in the law.

"Mouthpiece!" Walter was scornful. "Why, all these so-and-so lawyers 'ang together. Why, I see a picture the other day of two of 'em walkin' arm an' arm together – and they was on different sides in a murder! No so-and-so lawyers for me!"

"Moderate your language," said The Miller. "I'll tell Evans, though I don't know what he can do for you except to tip that you'll get time. In which case you'll probably get off."

Educated Evans, of Tarpin Lodge, Bayham Mews – he had a disconcerting habit of renaming his residence after big race winners – was indeed a friend to the poor and afflicted, in addition to being the World's Greatest Turf Adviser.

And at the moment he was riding on the crest of a wave.

Camden Town, which had lost confidence in the man and the prophet, was slowly regaining its faith. For had he not given in rapid succession:

> Argo! What a beauty!
> Argo! What a beauty!
> Argo! What a beauty!

together with

Mr Clever! What a beauty!
Mr Clever! What a beauty!
Mr Clever! What a beauty!

to quote his own admirable literature.

It was rumoured – mainly by Mr Evans, that the West End bookmakers were panic-stricken. People had come to his flat and paid him real money to encourage him in his good work.

The Miller walked up the wooden stairs which led to Tarpin Lodge, and found the one who described himself immodestly as The Wizard of Camden Town engaged in the study of the next day's programme. Evans received him gravely – as a man of property would receive a bailiff, or a successful author a reviewer; in other words, as somebody who was respected but did not count.

Briefly The Miller explained the reason for his visit. Evans shook his head.

"I've given up writin' out defences for common people," he said. "I'm too busy, as the well-known Sir Francis Drake said to the soldier when he was teachin' the young princes in the Tower to say their twice-times table. What with owners an' trainers an' what-not writin' to ask me not to tip their horses, an' what with me correspondents at Lambourn, Newmarket an' Epsom sendin' me yards an' yards of winners, I've got no time to disgrace meself with Walter Holl. What's he done?"

The Miller told him, and Evans made an impatient sound.

"The man was certainly a client of mine in the past, but whether he acted honourable or not I can't tell till I've seen me books. I'll see what I can do."

"What's going to win the Gatwick Handicap?" asked The Miller.

"Blue Nose," said Evans indifferently. "I'm not troublin' about that race – it's too easy. Give me somethin' hard, like the Victoria Cup."

"Blue Nose?" queried The Miller.

Evans went to his bed, turned over the pillow and produced a letter.

"Read that," he commanded.
The Miller read.

DEAR SIR,
With reference to your enquiry, Blue Nose has done no work
for six months and has a very bad leg.
Yours faithfully,
H HAGGIT.

"That Haggitt," said Evans profoundly, "couldn't tell the truth to
his doctor. What's more, he owes me one. So I wrote to him, knowin'
that whatever he sent me would be a lie. Blue Nose is money for
nothin'. Help yourself an' don't forget I've got to pay rates an' taxes."
The Miller was impressed.
"Telltale will win the Victoria Cup," he hazarded.
Here The Miller voiced the opinion commonly held by all keen
racing men. For Telltale had, so to speak, been flung into the handicap.
He had been left – also, so to speak – ten minutes in the Newbury
Cup and had been beaten a short head by a great horse. Ardent
sportsmen in Camden Town were going down to watch the race in a
fortnight's time to place their underwear at the disposal of the
receptive bookmakers and, if the truth be told, Walter Holl's divers
larcenies and felonies had been performed or committed with the
object of getting a little stock of money to invest in this gilt-edged
security.
Educated Evans scratched his nose.
"He *ought* to win it," he admitted. "He ought to be able to fall
down an' get up an' then win. But them bookmakers won't lay more
than twoses an' more likely it's be six ter four on the field an' twenty
to one bar two. And that don't pay me an' my clients."
He looked round cautiously, though there was no danger of being
overheard.

"You're in the lore, Mr Challoner; what about Dum Spyro? He's trained by Falston – he's the nephew of Lord What's-his-name, the highly celebrated judge."

"You mean Mr Justice Bellfont?" asked The Miller.

"That's him. Don't you ever get any tips at Scotlan' Yard? Don't judges put things in your way – they ought to. Where would they be without busies?"

The Miller chuckled.

"The judge doesn't give tips, you poor miserable man!"

Evans was deep in thought.

"If I thought Dum Spyro was on the job I'd take him to beat the fav-rite. But that Falston's so close that he's stuck together. He don't bet, but he wouldn' tell his own wife where he kept his shirts: he's that tight you couldn't open him with a pickaxe."

The Miller went away and brooded on the immediate problem of Blue Nose. He was, in a way, slightly amused by the perverted reasoning of the World's Premier Turf Prophet. So was the station-sergeant and several form-studying constables. When Blue Nose won that afternoon by the length of a street they were slightly annoyed.

Evans spent the greater part of the evening composing an address which Walter could read from the dock. He had composed many such: generally speaking, they began in very much the same strain.

"May it please your Worship. It was said by the celebrated Shakespeare, 'The quantity of Mercy is not strange,' therefore I ask your worship, in the terrible position I find myself, an innocent man dragged ruthfully to the bar of justice, to take a lenient view of a mere bagatelle committed under the influence of drink, that well-known curse."

The three hours spent in this labour were, however, so much wasted time, as he learned on attending the police court the next morning.

"Sorry, Evans," said The Miller, "but this will be an Old Bailey case. We found a lot of stolen property in his house, and he's certain to be fullied.★ He tells me he's done a bit of work for you in the past two years?"

This was true. Holl had earned many an odd shilling. He had run a few errands, scrubbed the educated man's floor, and once had distempered the walls of his bedsitting-working room.

"If you go up before the judge and say a few words for him, you might save him a lagging," suggested The Miller – a scheme which at first filled the World's Champion with quaking fear, but which afterwards had certain attractions.

Educated Evans had participated in many police court proceedings, but he had never yet attained the the distinction of making an official appearance at the Old Bailey.

By great good fortune, Holl was fullied in time to catch the next week's sitting of the Central Criminal Court. Kind friends, one and all, whipped round to supply the funds necessary to secure the services of that eminent barrister-at-law, Mr Chubble-Chine, a very young man who knew just as much of the world as can be viewed from the quad of Caius College, Cambridge, and Pump Court, EC4. Educated Evans, wearing his check trousers and nearly gold horseshoe tiepin, strolled into the hall of the Old Bailey, the observed of all observers.

"It's curious, Mr Miller," he said modestly, "how a feller gets known. All them people know me… I'm so to speak, the sinicure of all eyes."

"They think you're Woddle, the forger, surrendering to his bail," said The Miller coldly. "And listen, Evans: when you get up in front of the judge, don't talk too much – it's Bellfont."

Figuratively speaking, the ears of Educated Evans pricked.

"The highly famous Lord Bellfont – him whose nephew trains Dum Spyro?" he asked, and The Miller nodded.

"That's a bit of luck," said Evans thoughtfully.

"When he sees the kind of man he's got to deal with, I bet he'll ask me into his private room an' have a talk – "

The Miller's eye was cold.

★ Fully committed for trial.

"The only private room you'll ever be asked into," he said, "is one of twenty in the basement, which has a lock on it and a peep-hole where the warder can see that you're not committing suicide."

Nevertheless, Mr Evans was not depressed.

It was two o'clock that afternoon when Holl stepped brightly up from the bowels of the earth into the dock. He pleaded "Not guilty" in a chirpy tone.

At a quarter to three, Educated Evans walked into the witness-box and, having sworn to tell the truth, leant negligently on the ledge of the box.

"You are," said the youthful counsel, "a very well-known sporting journalist?"

Evans was momentarily staggered at this description.

"In a sense and in a way I am."

The saturnine figure on the bench glared at him.

"Are you or aren't you?" he rasped.

"I am, my dear lord," said Evans, and went on to answer questions which were intended to prove, beyond any question of doubt, that Walter Holl was between whiles a hard-working man, a good father and a kind and loyal friend. The counsel for the prosecution did not even trouble to cross-examine him.

Not so Mr Justice Bellfont.

"When you say you are a sporting journalist, what do you mean?" he demanded.

"The fact is, my dear lord – " began Evans.

"There is no need for you to be affectionate," said his lordship.

"The fact is," said Evans, a little wildly, "I'm what you might term the World's Champion Turf Adviser and Pronosticator. I'm the gentleman that gave Braxted at 20/1 – what a beauty, dear lord! Also Tarpin – "

"Oh – a tipster!"

It is impossible to convey all the scorn, derision, contempt and condemnation in his lordship's tone.

"Yes, my dear sir – my dear lord, I mean – I'm a prophet. As the well-known and highly respected John Bunions, the celebrated composer of Robinson Crusoe and his man Friday, said – "

"A tipster!"

His lordship's lips curled.

"A prophet an' turf adviser, dear my lord," murmured Evans. "The same address for twenty-five years; not one of them gone today and come tomorrer people. As the far-famed Lord Winston Churchill said, 'Jer swee – I'm here!' "

The judge leant back in his padded chair; the cold malignity in his eyes made Mr Evans shudder.

"You infernal rascal!" he muttered. When he was annoyed, he invariably spoke his thoughts aloud. "You robber; you ought to be in the dock!"

And then: "You have the audacity to come here to certify a man's character!"

"Yes, my dear lord," said Evans faintly.

"You sent out your inf – your prophecies as to what horse will win?"

"Yes, dear – my lord." Evans in his terror was swaying in the box.

"And you have the – really I – I am amazed at your audacity! Do you profess to be able to predict horses that will win races?"

Evans nodded – he hoped respectfully.

"I believe you are a swindler!" said the judge firmly. "I believe that you are obtaining money by false pretences."

The educated man saw the prison gates yawning wide to receive him. Cold perspiration trickled down his nose. The hands that gripped the ledge were clammy – the court spun round him.

But the unconquerable spirit which is latent in every prophet sustained him. In a last desperate effort to justify himself:

"The fact is, dear old – dear mister...my lord," he stammered, "it's easy. Now take Telltale – he can't help winnin' the Victoria Cup..."

"Not a ghost of a chance," muttered his lordship. "Not with Dum Spyro in the field..."

So low he spoke that only Evans heard him. Then, aloud, and with a stern look in his eye:

"Stand down, sir!" he said. "The fact that the unfortunate prisoner has nothing better in the shape of witnesses than a wretched swindling tipster, is proof of his friendlessness."

He let Walter off with a three months' sentence.

Evans staggered out of court like a man in a dream. The Miller spoke to him, but he did not hear. In Newgate Street he found a taxi and drove back to Bayham Mews.

That evening, Detective-Sergeant Challoner made one of his frequent calls at the Hall of the Prophet, and found Evans in his shirt-sleeves struggling with the patent duplicator that a child could work. Round and round the little cylinder was turning, and with every revolution there appeared a quarto sheet, wet with violet ink. In silence The Miller picked up a sheet and read:

EDUCATED EVANS
*The World's Champion Turf Profit and Racing
Adviser*
Owner of the following high-class performers
under both Rules:
RAW MEAT TOMMY HAKE SHIN SORE
EYEBALLS WIGGLE WAG JERUSALEM
MOKE

Educated Evans, commonly called The Wizard of Camden Town (same address for 30 years) has given some of the biggest selections the world has ever known.

BRAXTED 20/1! What a beauty!
BRAXTED 20/1! What a beauty!
TARPIN 11/1! What a beauty!
TARPIN 11/1! What a beauty!
Educated Evans begs to announce that one of the

BEST JUDGES OF RACING
BEST JUDGES OF RACING
BEST JUDGES OF RACING
has kindly given him the winner of
THE VICTORIA CUP

This horse has 21 lb. in hand of TELLTALE.
This horse is trained by
A RELATION
of the best Judge of Racing and
IS TRYING.
Send PO for 5/- to Educated Evans, Tarpin
Lodge, Bayham Mews.

"What is the horse?" asked The Miller.

"Dum Spyro," said Evans rapidly. "I had it from Lord Bellfont hisself – didn't you see him give me the wink?"

AN AMAZING SELECTION

There is no doubt at all that Educated Evans had a soft spot in his heart for ladies. And it is no exaggeration to say that ladies had a tender place in their hearts for Educated Evans.

As Miss Amy Hallsback – the beautiful barmaid at the Rose and Crown – used to insist:

"I don't care what you say, he's a nice man, and the way he lifts his hat to you when you meet him out, is a fair treat to see. He may be long-winded, and I dessay he is, but there's no getting away from his education."

"He don't let you," said her gloomy audience; "he fairly rams it down your throat! I don't believe harf he says about hist'ry. Take that bit about Bloody Mary – "

Miss Amy's cold eyes fixed him.

"As a bird is known by his note so is a man by his conversation," she said pointedly, and left Mr Lew Figtree spluttering protests.

It was the same with the beautiful Miss Birdie Rothman and the same with Mrs Grail, the proprietress of the Egg and Duck. They all spoke well of Educated Evans. He was holding Miss Rothman spellbound one evening.

"Very few people know," he said, "that the moon is a extinct volcano. How it got up in the sky is a problem that's known only to a few of us. Take rainbows. Quite a lot of people think rainbows are real, but as a matter of act they're an optical illusion. Take Mars: there's canals on Mars owin' to their bein' no trains – everything's got to go by water. Take the stars – "

49

"Lord, Mr Evans, what a headpiece you've got!" said the awe-stricken lady.

Educated Evans smiled modestly.

"It's readin' that does it," he said, "an' experience. Take Camden Town. It used to be a wild jungle full of savages that painted their faces with wood – "

"It's not much better now," retorted the young lady.

Mr Evans' dearest enemy was one Old Sam, as all the world knows. His age was variously computed between seventy and a hundred and he had the appearance of one who had been on nodding terms with Noah. If the Biblical parallel be permissible, his ark nowadays was the saloon bar of the Red Lion, whence he sent forth his doves full of hope and confidence. This ale-sustained ancient who had once been the veriest slave of Educated Evans, shuffling about Camden Town to execute his orders for a mere shilling a time, had developed, as a result of his lucky pin-pricks, an arrogance, indeed a truculence, which ill became one of his years.

"He ought," said Evans bitterly, "to be thinking about another world, instead of which he's pinchin' The Scout's nap and sendin' it out as private information! But I'll do the old perisher! I've got a bit of information for the Liverpool Cup from me Epsom correspondent that'll fairly put it across him."

"It occurs to me," said The Miller, "that your style and language have deteriorated since your absence from Camden Town."

Evans coughed – somewhat embarrassed. Any reflection upon his diction touched him nearly and sorely.

"He's not worth any better. He's a low, uneducated, guzzlin' 'ound!"

The tenderness of heart which was Educated Evans' especial property, together with an increase in the volume of his business, led him – unwisely as it proved – to employ an assistant, Mrs Arabella Bolton, whose husband at the time was away in the country: a thin, peaky-faced, discontented woman, with a wail against life and against that much of life which sustained her husband in his Dartmoor retreat. Evans, who subsequently had reason to be thankful for his charity, took her on out of pity. A client of his had told him about the destitute state of Mrs Bolton, and since at that moment there was a great deal of work to be done, Evans sent for her.

"I'm sure I'm obliged to you Mr Evings," she exclaimed. "It's very good of you I'm sure I was offered a much better job last week but I was sick and all that I couldn't take it" – she spoke without any commas or full-stops, and her speech in some ways resembled an Act of Parliament.

"What with Bolton took away and bringing disgrace on me which my father thank God don't know anything about it or he'd turn in his grave and two mouths to fill and his relations not allowing me a ha'penny-piece though they're well off his father being in the butchering business in Smithfield market getting money out of selling bad meat to poor people that it's a shame what do you want me to be Mr Evings?"

Evans explained, and the thin-faced Mrs Bolton sat down in the one rickety chair with a disparaging sneer on her face, and proceeded to open and sort out the letters which had arrived by that morning's post as the result of an advertisement which, in some miraculous fashion, Educated Evans had succeeded in getting into the *Sporting Chronicle*. Usually the *Sporting Chronicle* is more careful.

Mrs Bolton lived at Little College Court, which rather suggests the shaded quadrangle of some ancient house of learning but was, in point of fact, a cul-de-sac of microscopic houses, where babies were born every day and old people died every other week.

Her next-door neighbour was a Mrs Lube, who had the dubious distinction of being the granddaughter of Old Sam, who now lodged with her, and at this time was keeping her, her family, her husband and her husband's aunt. The prosperity which had come to Old Sam as the result of his miraculous tips was advertised in Mrs Lube's sparkling earrings and in the magnificent watch she wore when she went to the cinema. She was a great friend of Mrs Bolton's – having troubles of her own – and there were, so to speak, no secrets between them.

"Good Gawd, Mrs Bolton!" said Mrs Lube, in a hushed voice. "You don't mean you're workin' for that old 'ound, the so-called Educated

Evans? Educated indeed! Why, he don't know nothing. Giving 'isself airs and takin' the bread out of our mouths, so to speak, me an' my poor husband, my poor old grandfather, a man of his age, to be cast on the world for us to keep!"

"I've got to live," said Mrs Bolton, hardly knowing whether she ought to defend her employer or admit his delinquencies and deficiencies right off, and ready to take either side under provocation.

"Of course, I don't think no worse of you," Mrs Lube hastened to assure her friend. "But it's a bit lowerin' to have to work for that kind of daylight robber."

"I've got to live," repeated Mrs Bolton. "What with my old man being put away through drink and wimmin as I shall maintain to my dying day and two mouths to fill..."

"Come in and have a cup of tea, Arabella," said Mrs Lube, as a great idea flooded her dull brain.

And in the best parlour – which was also the only parlour and had been newly furnished out of the proceeds of Old Sam's prophecies – they sat down and had a good talk; and Mrs Lube was an expert pumper.

"Wait a minute, Mrs Bolton. Do you mind me seeing my grandfather? He usually has a cup of tea and a bloater about now?"

Mrs Lube hustled out of the room, went up the narrow stairs and intruded herself into Old Sam's bedroom. Here sat the prophet. He woke with a start, rubbed his bald head and blinked up at his granddaughter. She closed the door carefully and, in a hoarse whisper, passed on the information she had gained.

"...it's running in the Liverpool Cup on Thursday. He's had it from Epsom."

Old Sam scratched his bald head.

"Paddy?" he said thoughtfully. "Never 'eard of the 'orse. Is it a 'orse?"

"How do I know, grandfather?" rasped Mrs Lube. "I'll ask Alf when he comes home."

"What can I do?"

"Send it out, grandfather," said this representative of his progeny, who was the real manager of the business. "Spread it all over Camden Town – "

"He'll do it too," interrupted Old Sam.

Mrs Lube shook her head vigorously.

"No, he won't," she said darkly. "We'll settle his hash, grandfather…the low, common man, taking the bread and butter out of my dear children's mouths. I'm sure it's a struggle to live. If it wasn't for Alf's dole, we'd be out of 'ouse and 'ome."

Old Sam sighed. For three months he had been the most popular member of the family, but the return of Educated Evans had marked a crisis in his affairs.

"If something ain't done, grandfather," Mrs Lube went on, and there was a note of menace in her voice, "you'll be outside the Red Lion with your back against the wall, picking up a penny here and there."

Old Sam sighed again.

"Tell Alf to get it printed," he said, and was glad when the door closed after this dominating woman.

Mrs Lube's work was not done. A shrewd and thrifty woman, she had put a bit by for a rainy day out of the magnificent receipts which had followed the point of Old Sam's pin pricking the name of Charley's Mount in the Cesarewitch. Mrs Bolton needed very little persuasion.

"Five pounds in the hand," as she said, "was worth two or three in the bush," for it was by no means certain – indeed, Educated Evans hinted as much – that she had struck a permanency at Tarpin Lodge.

That evening, Educated Evans went forth in search of the one policeman for whom he had any respect, and he discovered The Miller, standing outside the Nag's Head, where he had been waiting for two hours in the hope of picking up an acquaintance of his, urgently wanted by Scotland Yard. Since his bird was not likely to fly thither that night, The Miller walked back down High Street and listened with scepticism larded with interest to the story Educated Evans told.

"Never mind about Roysterer, never mind about Dinkie," said Evans firmly. "This horse Paddy will win ten minutes. I got him from a man who's got a nephew in the stable. And, what's more," he added triumphantly, "I've seen him gallop."

"Have you been touting horses, Evans? " asked the surprised Miller.

Evans nodded.

"I go down and have a look at 'em now and again," he said indifferently, as though such events were an everyday occurrence. "Now nobody knows anything about this horse but me – "

"I seem to have observed that it's been tipped by several of the weekly papers," suggested The Miller.

"They're only guessing," said Evans meaningly. "I *know!*"

"What's that woman Bolton doing with you? You're not contracting a matrimonial alliance?"

Mr Evans turned upon him the gaze of a wounded fawn.

"I'm surprised at you, Mr Challoner," he said. "A man of my education. Why, the Queen of Sheeney – "

"Sheba," corrected The Miller.

"Well, whoever she was – she wouldn't tempt me. Nor would the celebrated Cleopatrick, who got her well-known needle through being turned down by the highly celebrated Nero, the far-famed Italian. If Mary Queen of Scots come into my room and said, 'Evans, what about taking me to the cinema?' I'd say ' 'Op it.' I'm done with women! Besides, she's a nagger."

"Mary Queen of Scots?" asked The Miller in surprise.

"No, Mrs Bolton. She's always got something to grouse about. If it ain't one thing it's the other, and if it's not that it's something else."

He certainly found Mrs Bolton in a grumbling mood when he reached home that night. She said she was ready to drop; she'd been turning the handle of the duplicator that a child can work, for three hours and she was in a condition of exhaustion.

The response to Evans' appeal had been a heavy one. There were no fewer than three hundred envelopes on the table, half of which were filled. Ever a lover of peace, the educated man gave her fair words and, more to the purpose, a promise of overtime; and together they finished the work, stuck down the last envelope and affixed the stamps. Evans looked at his announcement with a glow of pride.

> TARPIN LODGE,
> BAYHAM MEWS.

SIR,

Once more I am able to put you on to the Goods. Far-famed throughout every land and nation where the British flag has flown, the sun never sits on the name of Educated Evans, the World's Premier Prophet and Turf Adviser.

Today I send you a piece of information that nobody else has got!

> What a beauty!
> What a beauty!
> What a beauty!

You can go your maximum on

> *PADDY*★★★★

today – he will win in a canter.

> Yours truly,
> EDUCATED EVANS.

PS – Put me on the odds to 1/-.

"Rubbish and nonsense, I call it," said Mrs Bolton. Evans' smile was one of great superiority.

"You don't understand these things, Mrs Bolton," he said. "Naturally the turf don't appeal to women, though I've known ladies who've made fortunes out of my high-class selections."

Mrs Bolton sniffed. She was gathering the envelopes into packets and putting them into the pillow-slip which Evans had borrowed from her for the purpose.

"Post 'em in the High Street," said Evans.

"What about my money?" asked his assistant, more to the point. "I can't go toilin' and moilin' for a mere nothing with two mouths to fill."

Though her work was only for two days, Evans generously handed her three pounds.

"Is the overtime here?" she asked.

"Yes, and your lodging allowance," said Evans sarcastically.

He went to sleep with a feeling that he had done a good day's work. The information he had received about Paddy was undoubtedly reliable.

He was cooking his breakfast in the morning when a small and dirty-faced boy arrived with a small and dirty-faced note. It was from Mrs Bolton.

Dear Sir, I was took so bad when I got home last night that I can't come to work any more please send three pounds by bearer instead of week's notice yours truly

MRS BOLTON.

"Go back to your mother," said Evans, rightly sensing the relationship of the small and grimy child, "and tell her I'm Not Made of Money."

The little boy waited till he was downstairs and in the mews beyond the fear of pursuit, and made certain derisive noises which were very irritating to a man of Mr Evans' refined susceptibilities.

He had plenty to occupy his mind until the afternoon, and then he strolled forth to get a copy of the afternoon paper. It was a little disconcerting to find at the newspaper shop a small stack of Old Sam's Midnight Specials, and to be told that Sam had made Paddy his five-starred nap.

"The perishin' old plaguerizer," spluttered Evans, choking with indignation. "Why, that's the horse I sent out! He's got it from that woman Bolton that lives next door to him…"

His feelings were somewhat mollified by the arrival at that moment of a newspaper runner, and the discovery, in the smudged space, of the news that Paddy had won.

"Seven to two it is," said the shop-keeper. "I heard it on the telephone. One of the boys told me. They got that price from the blower round at the Arts Club."

Evans scratched his chin.

"The news must have got out," he said. "I reckoned it's be ten to one."

But a shock awaited him when, a little later, he strolled into the shop of a client.

"It won," he said laconically.

"What won?" demanded Harry Leek, the well-known furniture dealer.

"Paddy — I sent it to you — fear nothing!"

The furniture dealer frowned.

"You didn't send anything to me," he said, "or I'd have backed it."

Evans turned pale.

"Do you mean to say you didn't get my five-pound special?" he squeaked.

Not only had this gentleman not received it, but nobody else had received it, as Evans discovered when he made a rapid visit to four or five of his clients.

Pale with fury, he half ran to Little College Court and knocked at the door behind which Mrs Bolton had her habitation.

"Mother's ill in bed and can't see nobody," said an uncompromising young lady of fifteen.

"Go up and ask your mother what she done with them letters what I gave her to post last night," said Evans huskily.

"She ain't had no letters. She's not right in 'er 'ead — she's deleerious and nobody's allowed to see her," said the daughter, and pushed the door close in Evans' face.

"Is 'e gorn?" asked Mrs Bolton over the banisters. "Like his cheek, coming to my 'ouse!" she said, as she came downstairs, very fit and well. "That serves him right for trying to sweat the poor," she said.

"What are you going to do with the letters, mother?" asked her darling child.

Mrs Bolton ran her fingers through her untidy hair.

"They'll keep for a bit. I'll ask Old Sam."

She did not ask Old Sam because it was not her way to do anything she arranged to do. With Mrs Bolton things just happened; and she had forgotten the fact that underneath her bed was a pillowslip full of unposted letters, when on the Wednesday morning, she opened the door to see a familiar face.

"Good morning, Mrs Bolton. How's the world treating you?" asked The Miller cheerfully – and when he was cheerful something dirty was going to happen.

"Good – good morning, Mr Challoner," faltered Mrs Bolton. "You're a sight for sore eyes, I must say. Is it anything about my husband you want to know?"

"No, not exactly," said The Miller, leaning negligently against the door-post. "You've been working for Mr Evans, haven't you?"

She nodded, a sudden fear gripping her inside.

"I understand he gave you some letters to post – about three hundred, each with a stamp on it, which represents a total of about five pounds."

The throat of Mrs Bolton, a comparatively honest woman, went dry.

"Yes, sir, he did, sir," she faltered.

"Did you post them?" asked The Miller carelessly, his hard, grey eyes on hers.

"Yes, sir" – how she said the words she never knew.

"Are you sure?"

She nodded dumbly.

"Ah, then, I shall have to make enquiries at the post office," said The Miller, and took his leave with a happy nod.

Mrs Bolton closed the door and, staggering up the stairs, sat on her bed. Visions of the female equivalent of Dartmoor swam before her eyes. Going to the head of the stairs, she called in a hollow voice for her daughter, and Millicent – such was the name of this child – came up the stairs and listened to the horrid tale.

"Let's burn 'em," she suggested brightly. "Or" – as an idea struck her – "let's slip out and put 'em in the post tonight. Nobody'll see who posted 'em, and they can't bring nothin' up against you, mother."

It was a wonderful idea.

A gloomy Educated Evans strolled into the High Street, sad and depressed. All that morning he had avoided the busy haunts of men, gravitating, as was his wont, to the Thames Embankment; and now, with little interest in life, for he felt that his luck was baulked, he came back to the great highway with a feeling that fate had indeed baffled him.

The Miller, riding past him on his motorcycle, saw him, stopped, got off and came back with a beaming face.

"You old scoundrel!" he said heartily. "Fancy sending out a twenty to one winner! I've backed it, and you're on the odds to a shilling."

Evans' jaw dropped.

"Only got the letter this morning," The Miller took it from his pocket and handed it to the flabbergasted World's Champion. "You didn't tell me this horse was going for the Newbury Cup... I'll see you later, Evans."

Evans walked along High Street like a man in a dream, receiving, it seemed at every yard, the onrush of some admiring friend who crossed the road or flew from a shop to congratulate him upon his prescience.

For Paddy, who had won the Liverpool Cup at 7/2, had also won the Newbury Cup at 20/1! And the three hundred foolish people who had received the belated communication meant for the Liverpool event were blissfully unaware of what a providential tipster Mrs Bolton was. And Educated Evans, who did not even know that Paddy was entered for the Newbury event, received the congratulations with a modest smile.

"Yes... I was goin' to send it for Liverpool, but changed my mind...information pays in the long run."

A GOOD GALLOP

Alfred Robspear, a distant acquaintance of Educated Evans, called very early in the morning to borrow half-a-crown.

He was a raw, lop-sided man of forty-five, who had been out of employment for many years, since he discovered that, by calling every week at the Labour Exchange, he could draw enough money to keep his children and his favourite bookmaker from starvation.

"You don't get no half crowns out of me," said Evans firmly, and went down the wooden steps to fill the dustbins with some aged newspapers and a quantity of violet-stained rejects from the duplicator which a child could work.

Mr Robspear did not immediately follow. This, Educated Evans remembered later...

It was not the happiest day in Evans' life. It was, in fact, a morning of crisis when he surveyed his possessions and calculated skilfully and with accurate judgment the exact amount he could raise on his non-necessities. He had a library of books which included three annual volumes of *Racing-Up-To-Date*, a turf ready reckoner and five dog-eared volumes which had been presented to him by a client in lieu of the five shillings which Mr Evans had earned by his gift of prophecy, and which were supposed to be valuable, one at least being yellow with age and having 'f's' for 's's'. And it is pretty well known that ancient books with 'f's' for 's's' are sometimes sold for enormous sums.

Evans sighed and, gathering together his books, tied a piece of string round them and was leaving his room to carry the volumes to Jones' Renowned Marine Store, when a thought occurred to him

shrugs his shoulders, shakes his white head, strokes his patriachal beard and smiles.

"I can only tell you," he says, in his well-modulated voice, "that your horse is very well."

If the owner becomes a little too insistent, Mr Bolfort writes him a letter and asks him if he will kindly take his horses elsewhere. That is the kind of man Mr Bolfort is.

When his horses win, as they occasionally do, he is mildly surprised; but the surprise on the part of the public is not so mild, because his winners invariably start amongst the '20/1 others,' and low down punters, who have backed the favourite and seen it pipped a short head on the post, curse Mr Bolfort and wish his charge had dropped dead, yet console themselves by repeating: "When he wins I can afford to lose."

He had in his stable a horse called Fideles, which common bookmakers invariably called Fiddles, and Fideles was remarkable in that it had run thirty-five times without catching the judge's eye, or indeed any other portion of his countenance. Fideles was the property of Lord Livergrome, a gentleman of the old school who liked to see his colours in public. It would have cost him much less to have had those same colours carried around on a pole, but he preferred to see them on a jockey's back, and paid cheerfully the most expensive entrance fees.

By the curious workings of fate, John Bolfort was browsing in Camden Town and was standing at the counter of Jones' Renowned Marine Store and Second-hand Bookshop, examining a germ-infected copy of a very old book, when Evans came into the store, nodded jauntily to the untidy lady behind the counter, and put his books on the counter.

"I've got a few odds and ends here, Mrs Jones, you might like to buy," he said airily. "Me library's getting over-stocked. The books are valuable, but I haven't time to take 'em down to Christie's, the celebrated auctioneers."

Mrs Jones, with a look of disparagement on a face that was otherwise featureless, cut the string and turned over the books one by one.

"Four and six," she said laconically.

"Four and six?" said the indignant Evans. "Why, that there book's got 'f's' for 's's' in it."

"It's not worth sixpence," said the cruel Mrs Jones. "What's it about, anyway? What's a madrigal?"

"A madrigal," said Evans, with dignity, "as everybody knows, is a book about lunatics: one of the most famous books that's ever been published."

John Bolfort came out of his trance.

"Excuse me, sir," he said, in his gentle voice, reached for the book and, turning over the pages, uttered an exclamation. " 'Elizabethan Madrigals, collected by Thomas Scott' " he said. "I should like to buy that. Good gracious me! it's the book I've been looking for for years! What do you want for it, sir?"

Evans coughed. He hated to say too little for fear he got it, or too much lest he be assaulted. Mr Bolfort saved him the trouble.

"I will give you ten pounds," he said apologetically, and Evans nodded dumbly.

"You are a collector, sir?" asked Bolfort, ignoring the glaring Mrs Jones, who had been robbed out of £9-15-6.

"A bit of one," said Evans, recovering his voice.

Mr Bolfort shook his hoary head.

"Alas! I wish that I had the time to devote to that fascinating hobby," he said; "though I think I have the best collection of old English madrigals in the country. You must come down to Bolfort House one day and look over my library. I find most people are more interested in my horses than in my books."

"Bolfort House?" said Evans hollowly. "You ain't – aren't – you're not Mr Bolfort, the highly celebrated trainer?"

The highly celebrated trainer smiled sadly.

"I would rather be known for my madrigals," he said.

Five minutes later Evans walked arm-in-arm down Great College Street – with a trainer! With a man whose name appeared in newspapers, with a gentleman who could race horses every day of his life and think nothing of it.

"Yes, yes, you must see my collection," said Bolfort, who was interested in the subject of books to the exclusion of all else; who even regarded the shabbiness of his new acquaintance as a proof of his genius.

The Miller was patrolling High Street, Camden Town, next morning, when Evans crossed the road to intercept him.

"I got them trousis back, Mr Challoner," said Evans. "It was a bit of a joke on Robspear's part... It would have been awkward for me if I hadn't. I'm going down to spend a weekend with my old friend Bolfort."

The Miller looked at him suspiciously.

"It's rather early in the day for fairy tales," he said, "but I'll buy this one. Bolfort the trainer?"

"I'm spending a weekend with him," said Evans, coughing importantly. "As I've told you before, him an' me's like brothers. 'Evans,' he said, 'come down and see that horse of mine Fiddles'."

Evans coughed again, this time not so importantly. "I've been having a bit of trouble getting money in from clients – " he began.

"Why should they give you money?" demanded The Miller. "Except to get you out of the country?"

Nevertheless, when Educated Evans approached him with some urgency, The Miller parted. For there was this to be said about his educated friend, that he never forgot his debts.

The money was very necessary, for the fare to Marsh in the Moor was exorbitantly high, and the walk from the railway station would have been an immense distance if he had not been able to hire a taxi.

The next morning Evans woke up in a four-poster bed and looked round the enormous apartment with a sense of complacency. He had spent the night before drinking port and examining books which were Greek, Sanskrit and Cuneiform to him. He had skilfully led the conversation to the subject of racehorses, and had been as skilfully led back to the matter of madrigals and Gregorian chants. But this morning he was to see with his own eyes the interior of a real racing stable.

"Do you ride, Mr Evans? Why, of course you do," old Mr Bolfort corrected himself. "You were telling me how you won the Bengal Steeplechase."

Educated Evans turned pale.

"I haven't had a ride for years," he said, "and I'm a bit nervous about strange horses."

"Nonsense!" said Mr Bolfort. "I'll have a hack for you that is as quiet as a mouse."

What Evans at that moment wanted was a horse as steady as a concrete gun-platform, but this he could not state without a loss of caste.

The horse was waiting at the door. Mr Bolfort lent him a pair of boots and handed him a whip.

"I never use a whip," said Educated Evans tremulously.

"You'd better take a whip, sir," said the stable boy in attendance. "Old Toby shies at anything and he wants a couple of rib-benders before he settles down."

Evans took the whip in his trembling hand and looked again at the horse. It was an enormous horse: he could scarcely see over the top of it. How he got into the saddle he never knew. Before he realized what had happened, there was a huge mass of coarse hair wobbling beneath him, and he was clutching desperately at the saddle with one hand, following Mr Bolfort's hack as it moved towards the stables, which were half a mile from the house. Happily, Mr Bolfort was at first content to walk; but half-way to the stables, he called Evans to his side; and as though the horrible beast that the Worlds' Champion bestrode, understood his words, it broke into a most uncomfortable jogtrot which jerked every atom of breath from his educated body. Thereafter, however, the ride was a pleasant one, for Mr John Bolfort was also content to walk his mount.

"You'll see some nice horses," said the old trainer; "though I must confess that I'm not as much interested in them as my grandfather was. I love to see a horse looking sturdy, with his coat shining and a little flesh on his bones. I believe in treating animals kindly, as I would myself wish to be treated."

"That's what I always say," said Evans.

He was beginning to get used to the dangerous experience of moving through the air with his head some ten feet from the ground, and a little of the colour was coming back to his face.

"The curious thing about horses," mused Mr Bolfort, "are the likes and dislikes they have. Now I've got a horse in my stable that simply loathes old Toby."

"The one I'm riding?" asked Evans, feeling a certain amount of sympathy with anything that shared his utter dislike of the ambling beast beneath him.

"Yes, old Toby," Bolfort went on. "The horse in question is one called Fideles. The mere sight of that hack – "

He tapped old Toby on the nose, and old Toby did a violent shy, in the course of which, by some miracle, Evans preserved his seat, though not his presence of mind.

"The sight of old Toby," the trainer went on, unconscious of the panic he had aroused in the bosom of the World's Best Tipster, "drives Fideles into a fury. Now I've often tried to account for this extraordinary prejudice, but so far I have not succeeded."

"Do you mind if I get off the horse when we come to the stables – I mean before Fideles sees him?" begged Evans, large beads of perspiration on his brow.

"Certainly. You can't ride round the stables, you know," said the old man good-humouredly.

Happily there was a stable boy who seemed to understand horses at the entrance of the yard, and Evans slid down Toby's forelegs to the ground, his knees trembling beneath him, and for the space of two minutes he had the head lad to himself.

"Nice place, this," said Evans conversationally.

The head lad, who had the face of an aged man and the legs of an infant, growled something uncomplimentary.

"Going to see Fiddles?" he asked, and Evans' heart warmed towards one who pronounced the word correctly. "That 'orse ought to win a race, you know, guv'nor," said the head lad, "but Mr Bolfort won't give him a gallop – says it strains their 'earts! One good gallop, and old Fiddles would win that Richmond 'Andicap next week as sure as you're born!"

At this moment the trainer came back and conducted his guest round the stables. At the third door he paused.

"This is Fideles," he said, "and he's rather a wild fellow, so I wouldn't advise you to come inside."

He opened the top half door and revealed a ferocious animal whose lips curled back in a sneer at the sight of the man who had so often tipped him.

"That's Fideles," said Mr Bolfort. "Put him over the other side, boy."

It was only then that Evans noticed that there was a boy attached to the horse by an iron chain. At least, it seemed so.

"If I went into that box," said Mr Bolfort complacently, "he'd eat me. You wouldn't be in there two minutes, alive, Mr Evans. Whoa, boy!"

For Fideles had suddenly whipped round and lashed out with his hooves in the direction of the box door. Evans made a hasty retreat.

The inspection of the stables did not take a long time. Bolfort had spoken the truth when he said that horses did not interest him as much as madrigals. With some reluctance, but with the comforting assurance that the house was very near, Evans was assisted into the saddle of his hack and he and his host walked side by side out of the gate.

"I almost think that Fideles of mine would win a race, but unhappily he is such a brute that none of my lads likes to ride him, and the boy who does him – "

"Was that the boy who does him?" asked Evans in an awed voice, thinking of the diminutive youth attached by a chain.

"That is the boy that does him. He's too light: the horse would simply run away with him. He's such a brute..."

There was a clatter of hooves behind and he turned his head, and Evans, who did not dare to turn his head for fear of falling off, saw a look of amazement and horror in the trainer's face.

"Fideles!" he gasped. "He's after that hack of yours! Gallop, Mr Evans, for heaven's sake!"

Evans screwed his head round and caught one glimpse of the ferocious horse galloping towards him, followed by three yelling stable boys, and he almost fell off his horse.

Toby did not need to have spurs clapped to him, even if Educated Evans had had spurs to clap. With an unearthly snort he bounded forward. Evans clutched his mane and held tight. The horse flew past them; they were crossing a field at seventy miles an hour – or it may have been a hundred and seventy. It seemed more. A hedge loomed in front of them. Before Evans realized what had happened, he felt himself rise, fly over the hedge, still clutching the mane, his legs dangling helplessly, the stirrups striking his knees most painfully at every stride. He heard the thunder of hooves behind and, more by accident than design, saw the open-mouthed fury that pursued them not more than half a dozen yards away.

Through a field of cabbages, over another fence – how he maintained his seat he never understood – into a country road, past a car – or it may have been six cars – through a farmyard, twice round a haystack, with Fideles following, and then back towards the stable. Evans closed his eyes and waited for death as he saw his fear-maddened mount dashing, as it seemed, straight for a brick wall.

Toby stopped suddenly. Not so Evans. He described a wonderful curve through the air, and he had a sensation of flying, saw beneath him the top of a wall, then suddenly his eyes, ears and nose were filled with sharp ends of straw and he lay half-conscious.

Two stable boys helped him up, and he heard, in a dim, dazed way, that his horse was safe. He was not wildly elated at the news.

"Is Fiddles dead?" he asked hopefully.

But Fiddles lived.

On the evening of Easter Monday, Educated Evans sat in his room, a long cigar between his teeth, a look of infinite satisfaction in his eyes. There The Miller found him, at peace with the world.

"Congratulations, Evans!" he said heartily. "Fideles won all right – I got twenties to my money."

Mr Evans removed his cigar.

"You can thank me," he said simply. "He wouldn't have won but for me. I says to Bolfort when I see the horse, 'Bolfort,' I says, 'that horse wants a gallop. Let me lead him one gallop an' he'll win'."

"And did he let you?" asked The Miller incredulously.

Evans knocked off the ashes of his cigar.

"It wasn't a question of letting," he said. "The matter was took out of his hands."

The Miller did not believe him – but for once The Miller was wrong.

A HORSE OF THE SAME COLOUR

The two-year-old Hesperus was a grey. And the two-year-old Milikins was also a grey. And both their owner and their trainer were hoary-headed men who had grown grey with artfulness.

Mr Randolph Tooks (*the* Randolph Tooks) had two stables, one at Lambourn in Berkshire and one in Wiltshire, and to the Wiltshire stable he sent Milikins and to the Lambourn establishment he sent Hesperus, just as soon as he had bought these horses privately from their breeder. Only he changed their names, and when the stable boys at Lambourn were talking about the amazing speed of Milikins they were in reality talking of Hesperus.

Only the astute Mr Groom, the trainer, and the astuter Mr Tooks knew this.

"Hesperus" (wrote the head lad of the Wiltshire stable) "isn't worth tuppence: you can leave him out every time he runs."

He was writing to one of his punters, for naughty head lads sometimes have a few correspondents who will give them the odds to a flyer in return for information.

"Milikins is a smasher" (wrote a literary stable boy who supplied a plutocratic tipster with information). "We tried him yesterday at level weights with Hard Egg and Dontbelate and he smothered them."

"Be open and frank about these horses," said Mr Tooks, the wily owner. "If any of these newspaper touts come nosing round your gallops, don't hurt 'em — give 'em a drink. We'll enter Hesperus and Milikins at one meeting, I'll send my own boys to bring the horses on to the course, and we'll skin the ring."

It is not an offence at law or by the rules of racing to call a horse by any name you wish, so long as he runs in the name he is entered. There is many a high-sounding Derby winner who is called 'Bill' in the stable, and if the stable name for Hesperus was Milikins, nobody was hurt but the stable hands who, contrary to Rule 176, sub-section v, conveyed illicit information.

Educated Evans, the World's Champion Prophet and Turf Adviser, did not ordinarily interest himself in the thoroughbred racehorse, as a horse. To him, a horse was a name in the daily newspapers anchored to the column by a weight, the names of his owner — to which 'Mr' was affixed — and his trainer, who was just Jones or Smith without any mistering nonsense whatever.

But Mr Evans had smelt the early dawn of the gallops and seen the vast uplands of country places and had, moreover, felt the soul-stir which comes only to those who have sat on the back of a thoroughbred hack. In other words, he had once been the overnight guest of a real trainer, and the exhilaration of the experience had got into his blood and even found its way to his legs for from Isaacs in High Street he acquired a pair of riding breeches and gaiters.

But the most remarkable change that this experience of his had brought about was his passion for observation. He had been twice to Epsom and had shivered on the top of Six Mile Hill whilst innumerable horses that looked very much like one another came at an alarming pace towards him. He had been as far afield as Newmarket — and he made one most profitable visit to a spot which was somewhere between East Ilsley and Wantage. It may be explained that none of these journeys cost money, a friend and client of his, who did odd cartage jobs with a van that he had picked up for a song, giving him a lift whenever he was going near to a training centre.

These serious preoccupations of Educated Evans had not escaped the keen eyes of Camden Town. Mr Evans was again in favour. Even the carters at the goods yard, who had once – so it is said – bribed the driver of a shunting engine to run over him, took him to their arms. His detested rival, Old Sam, had been unlucky. Possibly he was using the wrong kind of pin to find winners, but certain it is that, when the ancient man walked abroad, his beard of many colours floating in the wind, disappointed punters said bitter things to him. The riding breeches and gaiters of Educated Evans were the final blow to Old Sam. He came to Evans' house one night, breathing hops and vengeance, but the Educated Man had gone down into Berkshire overnight.

Early the following morning Mr Groom, the eminent trainer, rode out on to the downs – his string of horses having gone ahead of him. Cantering towards the end of the trial ground, he became aware of a figure on his misty horizon and a van drawn up by the side of the road.

"Good morning, sir," said Mr Groom politely.

"Good morning, sir," said Evans, ready to bolt.

"Are you one of those newspaper gentlemen?" said the amazingly polite trainer.

Evans, who could not tell a lie, admitted that he was.

"Ah! then you'll see an interesting gallop," said Mr Groom. "I never object to newspaper gentlemen seeing my trials. What paper do you represent?"

Educated Evans mentioned a journal which would have reeled from Printing House Square to Fleet Street had it but heard.

"It's a good paper but the price is high," remarked the trainer.

"We're thinkin' of reducin' it," said Evans carelessly. "I was only sayin' to Lord What's-his-name yesterday, 'people won't *pay* a shilling unless you give away a pattern or somethin – ' "

"Here they come!" Groom interrupted as four dots came over the skyline and grew larger every second.

Evans knew enough about horses to see at a glance that the leader was a grey. It flashed past him four lengths ahead of the rest.

"Yes…very good," agreed Groom.

"No, I can't tell you its name – but it is the only grey I have in the stable. Good morning, Mr – er – "

"Evans," said the educated man airily. "You may have heard of me – the celebrated Educated Evans? Braxted…don't that recall nothing?"

"Were you named after him?" asked Mr Groom. The Master of Paddy Lodge, Bayham Mews, shrugged his shoulders.

"I'll write it down for you," he said, oblivious of Mr Groom's obvious indifference.

Drawing a fat fountain-pen from his pocket – purchased only a few days before from the shilling bargain counter of Pelfridge's – he inscribed his name on a piece of paper he found in his pocket.

"Look out!"

Evans heard the warning shout and stared round. The horses had been pulled up and were returning to where he and the trainer stood. The grey, still fighting for its head, was within a yard of him and as he looked, the animal spun round like a teetotum.

Pen and paper fell from Evans' hand, as he stumbled back. He saw a hoof smash on the pen and a spurting fountain of green ink leapt up.

"Keep away from him!" called the trainer sharply, and Evans retreated to the road. He did not even call attention to the loss of his pen.

"That horse didn't seem to like you," said the van driver, as his passenger climbed up.

Evans shrugged again.

"I'm cruel to horses – I admit it," he confessed. "He ain't forgot the hidin' I gave him last week."

Three minutes later he was being rattled towards Newbury, his mind seething with excitement. At the first newsagents he stopped and bought a copy of *Horses in Training*, and turned eagerly to that page which bore the name of Mr Groom's charges.

"Milikins, gr. colt by Grey Fairy – Mill Girl."

Milikins! Here was a tip, not from the boy that did him, but from his very own eyes!

The Miller had been out of town for four days, having gone to Paris to take over the body of Harry Elbert, the well-known fishmonger who, being in a precarious financial position, had packed up a parcel of his employer's money (The Deep Sea Fisheries Limited – The Shops with the Blue Tiles) and gone abroad with the young lady from Higgins the Poulterers.

He came back and, having safely hutched Harry, went in search of Educated Evans.

That learned man he found at his home, Paddy Lodge, and Evans was engaged in the comparatively innocent occupation of frying a sausage.

"Ever heard of Ptolemy, Evans?"

The World's Champion Turf Adviser shook his head.

"Tolly Me?" he frowned. "That's one of Bennett's hair-trunks, ain't it?"

The Miller spelt the word and the face of his host lit up.

"Oh, you mean Pet-olmy – heard about him? He can catch pigeons. He's runnin' in the Jubilee – "

"He's running in the Derby, and they tell me in Paris he can't lose."

Evans sniffed and turned the sausage with his one-pronged fork.

"There's a horse in the Derby," he said, with great deliberation, "that can fall down, eat a good meal, get up an' *then* win it! This horse was tried twenty-one pound better than Sansovino, belongin' to the highly popular Sir Stanley Derby, of Derby House, Newmarket – a personal friend of mine. I've written letters to him."

"That seems a pretty slight foundation for friendship," said The Miller dryly. "Do you call all the people your friends just because you write to 'em?"

"I do," said Evans significantly, "if they act honourable. Everybody don't act honourable. Twenty-one pun' eight shillin's, a basket of greens and a gramophone that don't work – that's all I got out of three hundred clients."

"It seems a lot," said The Miller, and Mr Evans sighed in resignation.

"I gave 'em Paddy, 20/1 – what a beauty! did I or did I not?"

"You did," said the officer of the law. "You sent it out for the Liverpool Cup, but the woman to whom you gave the letters refrained from posting them till Tuesday. In consequence of which you've got a reputation you don't deserve."

Evans shrugged.

"Maybe I'll get another next week," he said mysteriously. "Maybe, when a certain horse comes home alone, I'll get a reputation that won't be deserved too! Oh, no! Oh, dear no!"

"I hate you when you're sarcastic," said The Miller. "Come on! What is this come-home-aloner?"

But Evans was adamantine.

"I'm sorry not to oblige you, Mr Challoner, but I've got competition in my business. There's a certain party – no names no pack-drill – who's fairly doggin' me to get information, him an' his pretty granddaughter."

Educated Evans used 'pretty' in the offensive sense to describe Mrs Lube.

It was regrettable that Mr Evans was not of the temperament which makes secrecy possible. All Camden Town knew that the master of Paddy Lodge had a rod in pickle: its actual name he did not tell. He contented himself with hints.

Certainly he had hinted to such effect that he had aroused a considerable amount of curiosity and, at the same time, had provoked mean-spirited men to discover for themselves the identity of this wonderful horse that he was giving on Thursday and which, in two incautious moments, he had stated to one person, would win the Birbeck Two-Year-Old Plate at Gatwick, and to another, that it was a grey. When you know the race and the colour of a horse, and there are but two grey horses running, and one of those loudly advertised by every newspaper dealing with the noble sport of horse-racing, it is not difficult to arrive at a conclusion.

"That's it!" said young Harry Gribbs, examining the programme. "It's Milikins! It'll start at four to one on – that's a nice five pound special, I don't think!"

In other quarters the identity of the animal had been discovered. The Miller called round to see his friend.

"Evans, you're going to lose your connection, my lad," he said.

Evans was in an irritable, indeed a nervous, state of mind, because he had recognized his indiscretion. In the first place, his secret information was everybody's news. It was difficult to find a weekly paper that had not put a star against Milikins, except those that had put two.

"And obviously that is the horse you've been gassing about all this week."

"That where you're wrong," snapped Evans, and The Miller stared at him.

"But you said it was a grey; you said it was running in this two-year-old race."

"Never mind what I said," Educated Evans looked almost truculent. "Ain't I entitled to be diplomatical, the same as the well-known Gallypot, the French astrologer who, when he was asked if the world turned round, replied to the houghty dogs of Venice: 'It do and it don't.' Ain't I entitled – Good Lord-'mighty! – to use discretion and artfulness and cleverness? Am I supposed to carry me heart up me sleeve?"

"Calm yourself, Horatius," said The Miller. "I meant no harm. Only everybody in Camden Town thinks you're tipping Milikins, and even Old Sam thinks you're losing your dash."

"So-and-so and so-and-so Old Sam!" said the exasperated Evans.

"Be calm, Elijah!" said The Miller gently. "And what is that horrible green stuff on your fingers?"

"It's ink that I got for me fountain pen – it won't come orf."

"Nor will Hesperus," said Sergent Challoner, and Evans ground his teeth.

He went back to Paddy Lodge, Bayham Mews, slammed and locked the door, and sat for a quarter of an hour glaring at the notice he had run off on his duplicator.

BETTER THAN PADDY!
BETTER THAN PADDY!
BETTER THAN PADDY!
BETTER THAN PADDY!

I am sending you one today which can catch pigeons. I am sending you one of the grandest horses that ever looked through a bridal! This one I have touted with my own eyes and seen all its work day by day at great expense! This one is better than Paddy ever knew how to be. He will start at 33/1 and win in a canter.

MILIKINS – FEAR NOTHING.

And don't forget your old and true and tried friend,

EDUCATED EVANS.

Paddy Lodge,
Bayham Mews.

P.S. – Beware of imitations. The police have orders to take into custody any person, young or old, who plaguerizes my tips.

Evans had brought into the flat with him a bundle of weekly newspapers, purchased at the local newsagent's, and now he examined the sporting prophecies with interest and despair, as sheet after sheet revealed the implicit faith of the anonymous sporting writers in the superiority of Milikins.

"We have seen Milikins do several gallops, and we know that his trainer has a high opinion of him" (wrote Bow-Wow in the *Racing Watch Dog*) "and there is no doubt that he is a certainty for his race on Saturday, and we have every confidence in giving

MILIKINS."

Evans groaned with every fresh discovery. He realized, in some indefinable way, that his very reputation was at stake. Camden Town was waiting to sneer at him and he took a sudden and dramatic resolve. Very painfully, he wrote out a new duplicator sheet, substituting for Milikins the word Hesperus. That at least was a grey and was in the same race – for he was committed to a grey.

What did the sporting newspapers say of Hesperus? Even the *Saturday Sports Herald*, whose training correspondents tip every horse in the race, had little to remark in his favour. "Ours is no good," said the local correspondent.

Others were equally offensive. Evans groaned again. There was no help for it. Better to send a wild outsider, without a possible chance of winning, than sacrifice his fame for sagacity. Setting his teeth, he finished writing on the duplicating paper, and the bell of St Pancras' Church was chiming three before he climbed into bed, so weary that he forgot to take off his braces – a precaution he had never neglected before.

Was Camden Town agog at the news it had received? It was.

"Hesperus?" said The Miller, wrinkling his brows, and went in search of the tipster.

But Evans had left by an early train for the scene of the contest.

Mr Groom, the eminent trainer, was running both horses, he was glad to see; for a non-runner was almost as damaging to the prestige of a turf prophet as an odds-on favourite.

In what miraculous fashion Mr Evans contrived to get into the most exclusive enclosures at a race meeting, nobody has ever discovered. He is one of the few sportsmen in the world who has had the distinction of being thrown over the rails of the Royal Enclosure at Ascot. Among his other battle honours is the experience of being kicked out of Newmarket private stand twice in one day. It is certain he was in the Gatwick paddock, without the title which payment usually confers upon the patrons of racing.

Miller had a day off; his motorcycle had whizzed him into Surrey, and his profession procured him the same advantage in the matter of admission as Evans had obtained under different circumstances.

"What's this Hesperus you've sent out?"

"A horse," said Evans laconically.

"Does it run?"

Evans closed his eyes.

"It will run and it will win by the length of the Holloway Road," he said. "I've had this horse give to me by the boy that does him, and I've brought down twenty pounds to back him."

The Miller shook his head.

"Give the money to me: I'll mind it," he said gently. "You're ill, Evans. The truth is, you intended giving Milikins, and when you found everybody else was giving it, you switched over."

Evans raised his shoulders in patient protest.

"Them that laughs last laughs least," he said cryptically.

It was true that he had as much as £25 in his pocket. It was quite untrue that he intended risking so much as a penny upon Hesperus. What he did design was a plunge on Milikins that would bring some solace for the losses he would sustain over his idiotic tipping.

Just before the 4.15, he was leaning on the rail, watching the horses parade. There were two greys, but which was Hesperus and which was Milikins, he did not know. Educated Evans never recognized a horse until the jockey got up.

Just as the numbers were going into the frame, The Miller came hurrying to Evans and led him to a quiet corner of the paddock.

"Evans," he said, "there's some talk about these horses being mixed up: that Milikins is really Hesperus, and Hesperus Milikins. You told me you saw a trial?"

Evans nodded importantly.

"Then you can tell one horse from the other. Which of those two greys won the trial?"

Evans glanced back at the saddling ring, where the horses were slowly walking. Beyond the fact that they were two greys, he was quite unable to distinguish the trial winner, for two horses, as I have remarked, looked as much alike to Evans as two pairs of shoes of similar make and size.

And then there flashed across his mind a recollection of the alarming incident which had marked the end of the trial.

"Here, hold hard, Miller," he said agitatedly. "I can tell you in a second!"

He hurried back to the ring, followed by Mr Challoner, and presently the greys came along, one following the other. Evans glared down at their feet and then, with a gurgle of joy, he pointed.

"That's Milikins," he said. "See them green spots on his legs?… My fountain-pen…"

Incoherently he told the story of his loss, which was now to prove his gain.

"That's Milikins," he said. "He'll win by the length of Tattersall's…that horse is money for nothing," he went on, forgetful of his rôle of prophet, forgetful of three hundred unfortunate people whom he had begged and implored to back Hesperus, "…that horse could stand on his head and win."

"You daylight robber!" said The Miller softly. "Then you were bluffing?"

Evans threw out his hands in protest.

"A man of my position has got to fyness," he said simply, and The Miller was in too much of a hurry to ask for an explanation.

Evans went back to the ring again. There were the green spots on the grey's fetlock. He smiled triumphantly and, clutching his £20 in a hot hand, he hustled his way into Tattersall's, took £35 to £20 and climbed up the stand to see his money come home.

"I've got to get it some way or the other, Mr Challoner," he said to The Miller, who joined him. "Self-preservation's the first law of betting, and – "

"They're off!"

The start was a straggling one, but Hesperus – even Evans recognized Hesperus now – jumped off in front, was a certain winner at two furlongs, an assured winner at four furlongs, and actually did win by ten lengths.

"Hesperus?" said the dazed Evans. "The – the thieves and robbers! They've been and rung them horses on me!"

And then it slowly dawned upon him that, however much his pocket might have suffered at Gatwick, his reputation in Camden Town was considerably enhanced.

"Well, well," he said tolerantly, "it's a case of information v. guesswork. If I'd stayed at home I'd have made a lot of money. I knew they'd run this horse, and ii you hadn't put me off it – "

The Miller gave him one glance, which would have withered an ordinary man. But Evans was no ordinary man.

Said Mr Groom, the trainer, to Mr Tooks. the owner:

"Did you see that ugly little devil looking at the horse's legs? He's a tout or something and came up to my gallops. What did he do? Why, he dropped some green ink on Hesperus. I guessed he'd been sent to find out which was which, so I cleaned Hesperus – and a devil of a job it was – and put a few green spots on Milikins. Artful, eh? I tell you these newspaper chaps want a bit of beating!"

MIXING IT

Every great man has his sycophants partly because, realizing their greatness, they cannot hear too much about it, and partly because flattery produces largesse in some shape or form.

Educated Evans was a great man: he was the World's Champion Prophet and Turf Adviser, which in itself is a distinction that many a man would give his head to possess. He was also a scholar and an authority on all sorts of esoteric subjects.

You could never floor Evans with any kind of question, historical, astronomical, biological or anatomical. He was the only man in Camden Town who knew what an appendix was for.

And Abe Slow was his most vocal admirer. Abe was a bookmaker who had fallen on evil times owing to his honesty. He used to admit this.

"If I'd thieved same as…" – he named quite a number of limited liability bookmakers, and named them libellously – "I'd be walking about in my Rolls-Royce car but, Mr Evans, believe me or believe me not, I'd rather have my ear cut off than fiddle."

Evans believed him. At that particular moment he believed anything, for he was in his politest mood. A high stool was under him, the shining counter of the saloon bar of the Blue Horses was before him, and within earshot was the loveliest barmaid in Camden Town – Miss Bella, she with the diamond ear-rings and the wrist-watch.

"Very true, very true," said Evans, condescendingly and loudly. "How true it is, as the celebrated Mikel Vally, the well-known

Eyetalian artist, said: 'Honesty's a good servant but a bad master,' which reminds me."

The beautiful barmaid was wiping a wine glass, breathing upon it to obtain a better polish, but she was listening and Evans raised his voice still louder.

"Travellin' as I have in all parts of the uncivilize' world, Africa, Orstralia, Wantage an' other wild spots, I've often seen things that people don't know, such as lions, tigers, ostridges – where we get feathers from – kang'roos, elephants…"

The beauteous Bella stiffled a yawn and walked to the other end of the counter to serve a customer. Mr Evans shrugged his thin shoulders, and from there on the conversation became normal.

"I've had my ups and I've had my downs," Abe went on, "but if I'd 'a had a gentleman like you behind me I shouldn't be in my present position – good health, Mr Evans."

Evans nodded as his beer flowed down another man's throat. He knew, but preferred not to know, that Abe was once a street-corner bookmaker, with a limit of tenses and a strict all-in rule for doubles, trebles and accumulators. Even these restrictive regulations had not averted ruin in the year that Humorist won the Derby. Abe had paid out £47 10s. 0d. over that race without a murmur – partly because the two chief winners were Lew Davis, the celebrated middleweight, and Alf Sossino, who had done two stretches for biting policemen, and partly because he was an honourable man. This latter cause was, however, the smaller part.

"Have you thought any more about that idea of mine?" asked Abe, as he wiped his mouth.

Evans had thought a great deal. That idea of Abe's was in a way rather intriguing.

"A man in my position – " he began, but Abe arrested his objection eloquently.

"You've got the capital, you understand the game, you've got the information," he said rapidly. "I've got what you might call the book-keepin' ability. It's money for nothing, Mr Evans. All you've got to do is to stand up an' the money rolls in. You know the ones that are dangerous, all you've got to do is to say polite, 'Very sorry, my book's full,' an' lay the duds!"

"It's rather low," murmured Educated Evans, half convinced, "standin' up on a race-course an' makin' a exhibition of yourself."

Abe grew more voluble, more urgent as he saw his great idea gaining ground.

"Everybody knows you by name, Mr Evans," he said. "People will simply flock round you..."

The truth must be told: Educated Evans was seriously considering the possibility of 'mixing it.' To tip with the one hand, and to make a book with the other. It was delightfully simple and had been done before. And the prospect of standing up on Epsom Downs and shouting the odds was not altogether without its allurement.

Ever a dreamer, he had visions of a palatial establishment in Shaftesbury Avenue and a big rosewood office where he could sit smoking expensive cigars and drinking port wine, whilst an army of clerks dealt with stacks of bets, mainly losing ones.

"I'll do the clurking, you'll take the money – give me a quarter share in the book an' pay my expenses, that's all I ask, Mr Evans," pleaded Abe. "You'll come home at night with your pockets full of money..."

"I'll think about it," said Evans.

He had already decided when strife disturbed the harmonies of Brisl Villa, Bayham Mews, N.W. It was due in the main to A Certain Woman.

The straw-chewing representative of the Criminal Investigation Department whom Camden Town called The Miller, listened sympathetically to Educated Evans.

"She came round to me an' asked me what I meant by takin' the bread out of her children's mouth by givin' winners – Dio-meeds, what a beauty!"

"Long odds on," murmured The Miller, "if you refer to Diomedes."

"I can't help the price," retorted Educated Evans briskly. "That horse was give to me by the brother of the aunt of the boy who does him, but it got out."

"And what did you say to Mrs Lube?"

"I merely told her that business was business an' that what her grandfather did was nothin' to do with me. She asked me if I wanted to see her and her children in a home an' her husband rejuiced to workin' for his livin' like a common lab'rer. I told her I didn't care. And that's the result!"

He fingered his cheek tenderly. The skin beneath his left eye was slightly swollen and very blue.

"If she hadn't been a lady I'd have sloshed her!" said Evans, his voice trembling with pardonable annoyance. "But like King Alfred the Unready, I turned again an' counted six. I wouldn't hit her back even if she'd have let me. I sort of looked at her contemptchus."

"Where were you then?" asked The Miller.

"Under the bed," said Evans. "I had to go somewhere so that I didn't let my temper get the better of me. I ordered her out of my room. But the woman's got no sense of dignity."

"Take a summons," suggested The Miller, in his best judicial manner.

Evans coughed.

"I thought of doin' it an' told her so, an' she got the poker an' started waggin' it under the bed. But she didn't get me – I was firm with her."

"What on earth did you do?" demanded the astonished Miller.

"I got farther under the bed," said Evans. "I beat a strategic retreat like the far-famed Hinderbug, the highly celebrated 'Un. An' she got frightened after a bit. I told her what I thought of her – "

"After you found that she couldn't reach you with the poker?" asked The Miller.

"It may have been before or it may have been after," said the diplomatic Evans. "I told her that she wasn't educated an' ought to be ashamed of herself. An' she began to see that she had a pretty hard nut to deal with an' got out."

"I'll talk to her," said The Miller, who was something of a peacemaker.

"Don't tell her I told you." Educated Evans was alarmed. "I don't want her comin' round here – I won't be responsible for what happens."

"To whom?" remanded the police officer sardonically.

There was a great uneasiness in the Lubian household. Mrs Lube was angry and Mr Lube was both worried and irritable. He came home from the Blue Peter as many as three times a day to enquire into the sale of Old Sam's Midnight Special, a little blue card printed locally and enjoying – until Evans' return – an extensive sale at sixpence. On the back of this card and printed in very big type was the announcement:

Old Sam's Friends in the Training stables often send him a 11th hour tip which is sent by telegram to all clients who act honourable and send 10/– by P.O.

Eventually – why not now?

Send today – without delay.

It must be admitted that the latter urgent request was a blatant plagiarism, being pinched from the literature of Educated Evans, who in turn had lifted the phrases bodily from a highly respected turf accountant.

When The Miller called at the little house where Old Sam slept and had his meals, Mrs Lube was on the point of leaving for the cinema.

Her face fell at the sight of The Miller.

"Come in, Mr Challinger," she said graciously.

Sergeant Challoner, who was accustomed to having his name mutilated by people who invariably chose the wrong pronunciation, followed her into the over-furnished parlour.

"Now, Mrs Lube," he said genially, "what is all this I hear about your going to see Evans and raising a fuss?"

Mrs Lube blinked twice.

"As Gawd's my judge and if I drop dead this minute an' never utter another syllable, I've not so much as spoken an 'arsh word against the

Dirty Dog!" she said tremulously. "I went up to see him as one lady to another gentleman an' all I said, without the word of a lie, an' if I die this very minute, was: 'Excuse me, Mr Evins, but do you realize what you're a doin' of to a poor old man that 'asn't got your 'ealth and strength.' I says, 'an taking the bread out of my children's mouth,' I says, 'with your low common tippin' and sayin' "Beware of spurious imitations",' I says, 'an' look here,' I says, 'I know enough about you to get you ten years,' I says, an' with that he up an' insults me about my lodger!"

"You surprise me!" said The Miller. There had been certain rumours… "I am surprised," he said again, and Mrs Lube nodded.

"And he called my poor dear grandfather a beer-bitin' old 'ound! So naturally, bein' a woman with feelin's, I handed him one!"

"Naturally," murmured The Miller.

"An' the low, cowardly, sneakin' so-and-so − excuse my language, Mr Challinger, but I'm a woman and have got my feelin's − he got under the bed and yelled murder! If I'd only got at him with a − with my hands, I'd have skull-dragged him!"

Thereupon The Miller began to speak, no longer affably, but in the ominous fashion of detective sergeants, and what he said left Mrs Lube unrepentant but in tears.

She had recovered by the time her grandparent returned from lunch at the Red Lion, his nearly white beard waving in the breeze.

"…only a couple of pints, Amelia," he protested, "an' one of them was give me."

"Now listen to me, grandfather," said his buxom descendant. "This has gone on quite long enough. How many midnights do you think you've sold today − ten! You've got to rouse yourself up, gran'father; you've got to bustle round. I've got two Mouths to fill and Alf talks about sellin' the pianner. Me and him and you are goin' to the races tomorrow an' you've got, to hang round and Hear Something."

"Races?" gasped her relative. " 'Orse races? I don't know nothing about 'orses. I'd get run over."

"You're goin' to the Epsom races tomorrow," she said firmly. "I'm not goin' to allow that low, common potherb to say you don't know nothing about a horse except that he drinks water – that's what he said, grandfather, when he was under the bed – an' I'm goin' to take you down tomorrow. Alf's borrowed a horse an' cart an' Charlie Luce, the sign-painter, is getting some placards painted to put on the side. Alf says it's the only thing to do. He's a racin' man. He says you've got to advertise. All you've got to do is to sit round wearin' a top hat – I got one from the secondhand shop for ninepence. Alf will do the talkin'."

Old Sam was mollified.

"I can sit round in a top hat all right," he said, "if it fits."

"It's got to fit. I can put a bit of paper under the lining," said the determined female; "and we'll have a few bottles of beer in the cart."

"Ah!" said Old Sam. Epsom grew suddenly an attractive place.

Two mornings later, all the street in which Old Sam lived, gathered to see the resplendent cart which was to carry him to the field of victory.

"Now understand this," said Alf, the oracle, as he doffed his collar. "We've got to give a winner today or we're out!"

"What's going to win this race?" asked Mrs Lube.

"I don't know. Taping's a certainty, according to the papers, but it's no good giving short-priced horses. What we want is a sign. I dreamt last night of boiled mussels: is there a horse called Boiled Mussels running?"

They searched the programme, but if Boiled Mussels existed his owner had neglected to enter him for any event that day.

"What about asking Mr Dimitri?" suggested Mrs Lube helpfully, and her husband turned on her a disapproving eye.

"I don't want no lodgers interfering with my business," he said coldly.

Mr Dimitri was a shipping clerk employed by an Athenian firm, and occupied the room next to Old Sam. He was, it must be confessed, a constant source of friction between husband and wife, for he was young, fairly good-looking, and had nice manners.

"I thought of asking him to come down with us," suggested Mrs Lube.

Her husband's eyebrows rose.

"If he goes, I stay at home," he said, and Mrs Lube, who could be very violent, became so.

"All right, all right," said Alf, in alarm, for he had, on more occasions than one, been forced to take the cover which had so well served Educated Evans. "Don't let's have any argument."

And so Mr Dimitri, who had already arranged to go by train, being a thrifty man, leapt at the opportunity of being conveyed free of all charge to Epsom Downs, with the chance of cold meat sandwiches and bottled beer thrown in. Thus they progressed through Streatham and Ewell, amazing all beholders; and thus they came, Mrs Lube furtively holding her lodger's hand – for her husband was driving and her grandfather was asleep – to the Downs.

To Educated Evans, the day on which the Great Metropolitan Stakes was decided had been a day of splendour and glory. For the first few minutes of his experience, he was embarrassed, alike by the new satchel he carried over his shoulder, and by the bundle of tickets which he gripped in his moist hand. But the novelty appealed to him. The result of the first race in which, by some miracle, nobody amongst his ever-growing list of clients backed the winner; no less than the delightful consequences of the second race, where the only person who did back the winner never troubled to claim his money, gave him a confidence which might have had disastrous consequences, but for his attendant book-keeper.

"Don't go shouting twenty to one the field, Mr Evans," begged Abe, beads of perspiration on his face. "It's all right now, because they think you're kidding."

"What shall I say?" asked Evans.

"Say 'Five to one bar one'," said the practical Abe.

"What do I bar?" asked Evans, interested.

"Anything they want to back," said Mr Slow.

He had behind him, supported on two sticks, a banner, painted overnight:

EDUCATED EVANS

The World's Famous Turf Accountant
No way barred   No limit.
Same address for thirty years.

And possibly it was true that his fame had gone abroad, for a stream of punters flowed steadily in his direction, and his satchel grew heavy with illicit silver. Evans went home that night from Tattenham Corner Station, sitting on his bag, and spent a delirious hour counting his gains.

"What do you think of it, Mr Evans?" asked his partner anxiously.

"Money for nothing," said Evans. "If Screw had won instead of Brissell, I'd have been able to retire. We'll settle up tomorrow, Abe."

Mr Abe Slow looked dubious.

"Better settle tonight." he suggested. "That's the custom in the profession."

Educated Evans gracefully bowed to the custom and paid out one quarter of his winnings.

He was now so engrossed in his new occupation that he almost forgot to send out his Five Pound Special, and would have done so for the City and Suburban had not The Miller happened along providentially.

"Taping is a cert," said Evans. "It's waste of money to send it out."

It was fortunate for all concerned that, having passed this piece of information on to one who received it with every evidence of scepticism and scorn, Evans had not time to set in motion the duplicator which a child could work, and Camden Town was deprived of an excuse for blasphemy.

A fair morning, with a chill wind blowing; the green, rolling Down, and a sky flecked with light, vaporous clouds; and a song in the heart of Educated Evans.

The crowd was bigger than on the previous day. New clients recognized him with a smirk. One helped to erect the banner with the strange device, and was rewarded. Evans examined the book with a professional air, rustled the cards between his fingers, and:

"I'll lay on the City! Four to one Taping, four to one Taping. Ten to one De Orsey, ten to one De Orsey…"

And then he stopped, as his eyes fell upon a horrific sight. Near to his pitch a waggonette was drawn up, and its emaciated horse was being released from his work of bondage, preparatory to being allowed to feed, free of all cost, on the grass provided by the Epsom ratepayers. It was an ancient waggonette; the weather-worn sides were covered with linen streamers, excitingly inscribed; whilst diagonally, and supported by two clothes-props on the cart, was a banner even more urgent and boastful than Mr Evans'.

EDUCATED SAM
The One and Only Camden Town Turf Prophet
and Adviser!
Inventor of the Midnight Special
PADDY   What a beauty!
What a beauty!
Beware of Imitators!!!

The placards on the sides were to the same effect.

"Educated Sam!" gasped Evans, growing purple. "Look at the old perisher!"

Seated in the back was the patriarchal figure of Sam himself, his whiskers crumpled on his bosom, his mittened hands clasped on his stomach, a hat a size or so too large crushed down over his ears, for he was sleeping peacefully, despite the proddings of a red-faced female in black silk.

"Wake up, grandfather," she said sharply. "You're 'ere."

Old Sam opened his eyes and stared round.

"Wake up, grandfather. Look, there's the race-'orses!

He glowered owlishly at the course, where half a dozen gaily attired riders were cantering up towards the five-furlong post.

"Got the cards ready, grandfather?" Mrs Lube was visibly agitated. "Go on, Alf, say a few words."

Alf was a stocky man with ginger hair and a drooping ginger moustache. He was something of an orator, having sold patent medicines in various markets in the days of his youth. He got up on the driving seat and became talkative, and Evans listened spellbound.

"Educated Sam!" he groaned hollowly. "Well, of all the sauce…!"

And then a brilliant idea struck him.

"Friends one and all!" his strident voice might have been heard in the grandstand, half a mile away. "This boozing old 'ound is trying to rob me of my living! He's no more educated that I – than you are. I'll lay twice the market odds against anything he tips."

Mrs Lube listened aghast. She climbed up the cart by the side of her drowsy ancestor.

"Go on, grandfather," she hissed. "Tip something."

Old Sam pondered a moment, stroking his beard.

"What's running?" he asked cautiously.

Alf, the barker, turned with a marked card.

"That sounds good – tip that."

"Not for this race, grandfather," his intelligent grand-daughter protested. "Tip it for the City. If you give one for this race and it don't win, you'll get no more customers."

"What about Taping?" asked Alf anxiously.

"Look at 'em conspiring together!" sneered Evans raucously. "They've never so much as seen a race-horse wag his tail…!"

So excited was he that he did no business on the first race, which was well for him, for a hot favourite won; and little business on the second race. It was only when they began betting on the City and Suburban that he came to realize his vanishing opportunities.

"What about De Orsey?" asked Old Sam. "He won a race the other day."

"A selling race," said Alf.

"He won a race," said the old man doggedly. "I see it in the paper. De Orsey!"

Alf and his wife exchanged glances.

"Taping won a race, too," said Alf.

"And it's easier to write, grandfather," said Mrs Lube, who did most of the clerical work.

"De Orsey," murmured Old Sam, and dozed off again.

Suddenly Mrs Lube uttered a squeak and pointed to their guest. "Greek...you married?"

Mr Dimitri's mouth was full of sandwich, but he shook his head.

"Greek Bachelor!" screamed Mrs Lube, purple in the face. "Go on, Alf – bark it!"

Alf was a good barker, and an example of his style may not be out of place.

"...You see before you one of the grand old men of the turf. He's looked after more 'orses than any trainer going" (which was true, for, in the days when horses were not a novelty, Old Sam – then a boy – drew water for them at the Red Lion for a penny a time, until some interfering society put up a horse trough, thus robbing the poor of their livelihood). "Take a look at him, and tell me, ladies and gentlemen, if a man like that could tell a lie! Old Sam is one of the most famous educated men in the country. He's writ books – "

"You're a liar!" roared the exasperated Evans from his pitch. "He can't write his own name, the thievin' old gin-hawk!"

"He's writ books," said the unperturbed Alf, watching with some satisfaction the spectacle of Educated Evans dancing from one foot to the other in his impotent rage. "And they've been bought and sold, as is well known. He's come down here to give you the winner of the City from information received..."

When the first of the tips came to Educated Evans. he laughed long and scornfully.

"Greek Bachelor? I'll lay you fifty to one," he said recklessly. "I'll lay anybody fifty to one Greek Bachelor!" he roared. "I'll lay 'em a hundred to one Greek Bachelor. That horse ain't got no more chance of winning this celebrated race than the far-famed Cleopatra, the well-known needle-maker. I'll lay any price you like Greek Bachelor – "

"Here, what are you doing?" asked Abe, in a ferocious whisper. "You can't go laying fifty to one against horses."

"I'll lay a hundred to one," said Evans rashly. "Come on – roll up…an 'undred to one…!"

Evans in the days of his youth had been a runner. He did not run as fast as Greek Bachelor, but he beat his field by a longer distance. He ran into the landscape, so to speak, and by-and-by that portion of the howling mob which had not taken his satchel and divided his money, gave up the chase and went back to the sport of kings.

Abe Slow who, belying his name, was just behind him, shouted the news, but still Evans ran and did not stop until he staggered up to the gates of a great mansion. Here he collapsed, and when Abe came up to him Mr Evans was receiving first aid from two uniformed attendants.

"What's this place?" he gasped, as he opened his eyes.

"Banstead Mental Hospital," said one of the men.

Abe Slow's lips curled.

"You don't want to go no further, Evans," he said bitterly. "This is your natchral 'ome!"

THE FREAK DINNER

All the world knows Frithington-Evans. At least, all the sporting world knows him. Even his educated namesake had heard of him. Mr Frithington-Evans was an extremely rich young man, an owner of race-horses and a pet of a certain class of people who did not work for their living, and who were sometimes described as 'the smart set,' occasionally miscalled 'society,' but more frequently referred to as 'that lot.'

Mr Frithington-Evans had so much money that he could have well afforded to race his horses honestly. But deep down in the slither of spirituality which he called a soul, he had a rooted objection to anybody making money but himself and his friends. He was by nature suspicious, changed his trainer as a rule twice a year; and when he found that somebody was backing his horses, employed a detective agency to discover who this miscreant was and if, by any chance, the unfortunate punter happened to be in Mr Frithington-Evans' employ, he was summarily dismissed.

Amongst his friends was Lady Mary Herban, a beautiful young lady, who was received in the homes of all broad-minded people. They qualified for this description when they received her. It was after Mr Frithington-Evans had won a nice little race in the north, with a horse that had 21 lbs. in hand, and which had started at 100/8. that Lady Mary suggested the dinner. Frithington-Evans wriggled and complained about the expense.

"Don't be so mean, Frithy," said Lady Mary severely. "You backed that horse s.p. with every unfortunate bookmaker in England – "

"I put you in," he pleaded. "You won a packet!"

"I know you put me in, and now you can stand the dinner. We'll have a real racing dinner, with jockeys and bookmakers, and we'll have canvas stretched on the dining-room walls and painted to look like Pontefract race-course."

Frithington-Evans turned pale and rattled his keys.

"That'll cost a lot of money," he said. "And I hate freak dinners anyway! Look here, Mary, let's wait until − well, I've got a nice little coup that's likely to come off at Chester."

"We'll have it now," said Mary scornfully; and since they were very good friends indeed − Lady Mary's husband being abroad and wholly indifferent − the dinner was arranged.

It is very trying for a man of delicate susceptibilities to meet the rebuffs and insults of common people, and the other Mr Evans never displayed his fine qualities to greater advantage than when he met with a smile, in which contempt and mysterious understanding were blended, the ill-printed placards which decorated almost every newsagent's shop in Camden Town:

IF YOU WANT THE BEST TIPS
OLD SAM HAS THEM!

Greek Bachelor!
Greek Bachelor!
Greek Bachelor!

£100,000 paid to any Charity if it can be proved that Old Sam did not tip Greek Bachelor for the City and Suburban.

Don't go to Educated Welshers − Go to the Grand Old Man of Camden Town.

Educated Evans could not afford to smile. Indeed, it was a painful physical effort to smile at all. Nevertheless, he met these vulgar attacks upon his probity with a loftiness which did credit, as some said, to his noble spirit but, as others claimed, to the thickness of his hide.

"Mixing it, Mr Challoner," he explained sadly, "always leads to trouble. As Looey the nineteenth, him that had his napper cut off in Paris, France, said as he was ascending the scaffold: 'They may 'ang me, but they can't prove I killed the little princes in the Tower.' And that's my position, Mr Challoner. I'm being persecuted like the celebrated Hougemonts, who was massacred in Batholomew's Hospital; but I'm too much of a gentleman to mind. It's breed that counts every time."

"It was very unfortunate," said The Miller sympathetically. "But whatever induced you to make a book?"

Mr Evans made a gesture of indifference. His brave heart would not allow him to reveal the despair which had settled on him. For the story of his Epsom folly had run like wildfire through Camden Town. Clients had written him insulting letters; he had been ordered out of the saloon bar of the Red Lion by a flaccid landlord who had uttered, in stentorian tones: "We don't want no welshers here." Even his thick-and-thin clients had deserted him.

"The public's fickle," he said philosophically. "And after Paddy! What a beauty, what a beauty; And Diomeeds – !"

Evans went home with an aching heart to Brisl Villa – still over a stable in Bayham Mews – locked the door and sat down in the airless, ill-furnished room, his head between his hands, his bruised spirit incapable of initiating the least movement. He heard the sound of light feet on the wooden stairs outside, but he did not raise his head. There came a knock, and another; and, arousing himself, he walked apathetically to the door, pulled back the bolt and flung it open.

"What do you want – " he began, but got no farther, and stood staring at his visitor.

She was slim and very pretty, and dressed with a simple elegance that took Evans' breath away. He did not recognize Lady Mary Herban, because he was no student of the illustrated weeklies which portray the higher branches of society in their moments of ease and recreation. If he had been such a student he would have seen pictures of Lady Mary, sitting on a shooting stick, pigeon-toed, at point to point meetings; he would have seen studio portraits of her singly; in fact, it would have been very difficult for him to have missed Lady Mary, who appeared in these high-class publications almost as frequently as the advertisements.

Her smile was a dazzling one; she exuded a faint perfume which went immediately to the head of this educated man.

"May I come in?" she asked sweetly.

"Certainly, ma'am," stammered Evans, and she followed him into the bare room.

"You are Mr Evans, aren't you?"

He nodded dumbly.

"I am Lady Mary Herban, and I am wondering if you can help me."

"Certainly, my lady," he gasped, when he could find his tongue at all.

"We are giving a racing dinner on Monday, and we are having a representative of everybody in the sporting world. We have a bookmaker who will lay us the odds, and we thought it would be an excellent idea if you would care to come as a tipster?"

Evans coughed. The word chilled him.

"I'm not exactly a tipster, me lady," he said. "I'm what you might term a Sporting Prophet. This is what you might call my office."

The tumbled bed belied him.

"We could pay you well, Mr Evans," said her ladyship, who was quite indifferent as to whether this was the office or the boudoir of the world's most famous turf prophet. "The dinner will be at my house, 104 Grosvenor Square, and we're having the room arranged like a race-course. Everybody will wear morning dress, and Lord Ferrerby is bringing two horses with their jockeys. We do so hope, Mr Evans, that you will be able to help us."

The head of Educated Evans was in a whirl. He expected the day to produce little that would assuage his misery; and here, by some beneficent working of providence, he found himself plunged as it were into the vortex of high society.

"I'll certainly do anything I possible can. You'd like a tip for the Derby? Zionist is a cinch. That horse could fall down, get up and then

win. Don't talk to me about Picaroon; don't talk to me about El
Sassik; don't talk to me about Con – whatever his name is. Zionist
could fall down – "

"I know, I know," said Lady Mary soothingly. "Then I take it you
will come, Mr Evans? I will give you ten pounds now and ten pounds
on the night. Here is the address. When you arrive at the house will
you ask for my butler, and he will take you to a room where you can
dress. We should like you to wear something rather loud. You don't
mind, do you?"

Evans did mind. He hated loudness. He preferred, and said so, to
wear his check trousers with white spats and a classy green tie, with
horseshoe complete. To his surprise, Lady Mary agreed that that would
be a more suitable costume.

As she was taking a graceful adieu –

"Hold 'ard, my lady. You don't mind me saying that I've been
engaged as private tipster to your ladyship?"

"Not at all." Lady Mary seemed to be delighted at the prospect.
She hated publicity but liked to be talked about.

For an hour after she had left, Evans sat trying to put in order his
scattered thoughts, though it was rather like trying to catalogue the
sparks at a fireworks display. And then the possibilities of this
adventure began to take hold of him. There would be present at the
dinner lordly owners, possibly aristocratic trainers, certainly a jockey
or two. He might stock himself for a year on the information to be
gleaned at that remarkable banquet.

Putting on his hat he hurried forth in search of his oracle; and The
Miller, who had had a pretty unpleasant morning at the police court,
was not at first in a mood to advise him.

"Lady Mary Herban!" he said. "That woman would raid herself in
a vice den to get her name in the papers!"

Educated Evans began to look upon life from a new angle. The
jauntiness returned to his step; the smile which greeted the placarded
slanders of Old Sam became natural. Here he was, private turf adviser
to the aristocracy! He had been chosen, of all the thousands of

members of his profession, to represent the fraternity. It was not unpleasing.

He made at least two visits to Grosvenor Square, and from the opposite side of the street regarded with rapture and awe the magnificent mansion which held so rare a jewel as Lady Mary Herban, and in which he would figure, to the confounding of his detractors and the utter annihilation of his senile rival. Such things are reported in the newspapers. On the following morning he would see:

"Among those present at Lady Mary Herban's select and aristocratic party was the well-known Educated Evans, whose celebrated tips are so popular just now. Mr Evans, a tall, good-looking man in the early forties, replying to the toast of his health, said – "

The relatives of Old Sam, not unnaturally jubilant at the turn of fortune's wheel, had at the same time no doubt about the elasticity of their enemy.

To them came a distorted rumour of Mr Evans' noble patronage.

"That feller would swank hisself into Buckin'ham Palace," said Mrs Lube. "Alf, don't let him out of your sight! If he's goin' to a lord's party, as he says he is, he's bound to get soused and you ought to be able to get anything out of him!"

"He ain't goin' to any party!" said her husband contemptuously. "It's all talk!"

But Mrs Lube was not of that opinion.

"The Miller says he is – he told a friend of mine. Alf, that man would swank hisself into the Bank of England. Watch him!"

Little did Mr Evans know that from then on he was under observation.

It was seven o'clock on a pleasant spring evening when he descended the area steps in Grosvenor Square – Mr and Mrs Lube watching furtively from the corner of the square – and was received somewhat haughtily by Lady Mary's butler. Lady Mary's butler,

Simmings, was less impressive than ordinary by reason of the fact that all the staff had been ordered to array themselves in sporting attire. And Mr Simmings was certainly too stout for a jockey.

"Come in, come in," he said testily. "Henry, show this man up to the dressing-room...lot of stuff and nonsense! I never heard of such rubbish in my life..."

Henry, who was also dressed as a jockey – and rather fancied himself, for he was thin and had legs like straws – led the way up the stairs into the big ball.

"Want to see this show before it starts?" he asked and, pushing open the door, Evans saw an amazing sight.

The room had been converted into a race-course. The table, which ran down the centre, was covered with green cloth, and a winning-post had been erected at one end where Lady Mary was to sit. The walls had been converted by the scene-painter into an idealized race-course. The floor was covered by a rough green cloth, a judge's box, real rails and a saddling bell had been added to the room.

"They talked about bringing 'orses here," said Henry, "but they can't get 'em up the steps. You're a tipster, ain't you? What d'you know?"

Evans thought it was a moment to assert his dignity.

"I'm Mr Evans, the celebrated Turf Adviser," he said, with a touch of hauteur, "and as the celebrated Richard Cower de Lion, the well-known Gay Crusader, said to his brother, the Duke of Clarence, who was drowned in a bottle of claret: 'You keep your place and I'll keep mine'."

The impressed Henry handed him over to one of the men hired for the day who, alone, were dressed like civilized waiters. He was taken up to the third floor where, as he understood from Henry, he was to wait until he was called for. The gloomy, middle-aged man who escorted him to his room had views of a communistic type.

"If the money these 'ere burjoises were spending on this kind of muck was give to the poor, Comrade, this'd be a land fit for 'eroes to live in. But the day is coming," he added darkly, "when the burjoises will know all about it!"

"Who are they?" asked Evans, a little hazy.

"It's them that's got what you ain't got," was the cryptic reply.

Henry, the jockey, came up to see him; and Evans learned that he would not be required until half-past nine, when the dinner was over and he was left to rehearse his speech, which began:

"Ladies and gentlemen, – Educations, as everybody knows, is one of the grandest things in the world, and I stand before you today, an exposition of erudition and brain-work versus guesswork and picking 'em out with a pin..."

From below, when he opened the door, came the sound of revelry and laughter. The dinner had begun, and he paced the little room, repeating his speech, stopping now and again to fasten his white spats, which constantly came undone... There was a knock at the door: it was the socialistic servant, and he had in his hand a telegram.

"They ain't half goin' it downstairs," he said gloomily. "Wine flowin' like water! Little do they know what's waitin' 'em. This is for you."

Evans took the telegram from his hand: it was addressed "Evans, 104 Grosvenor Square." He opened it in wonder. Only The Miller knew he was attending this dinner party.

The wire was addressed from a little training centre west of Newbury, and it had been handed in at one o'clock that day, but apparently had been readdressed.

Evans, 104 Grosvenor Square. Tried Longlegs a certainty advise you run him Wednesday and have a good bet.

It was signed with the name of Mr Frithington-Evans' latest trainer.

For a long time the educated man did not understand his good fortune, and then he began a frantic effort to lick down the torn flap.

"This is for another gentleman," he said, "not for me. Take it down to him."

"One of the burjoises?" asked the waiter, with a sneer.

"He's worse than that," said Mr Evans.

Longlegs! he thought, as the door closed on the hired waiter. What a chance to rehabilitate himself with the sceptics of Camden Town! He had hardly reached this conclusion when the door was flung open violently, and a red-faced young man exploded into the room.

"Here, you fellow, what the devil do you mean by opening my telegrams?" he demanded wrathfully. "This was addressed to me."

"My name's Evans too," said Evans gently. "Perhaps we're related. We've had some very flighty people in our family, my uncle Joe – "

"Did you read it, confound you!" roared the agitated Frithy.

"I certainly read it – " began Evans.

"Oh, you did, did you?" said the gentleman between his teeth and, before Evans realized what had happened, the door had slammed and he heard the click of the turning lock.

Frithy flew downstairs. Lady Mary was waiting in the hall.

"Why on earth did you dash away? We're only just beginning – "

"That – that – that..." spluttered Mr Frithington-Evans pointing dramatically up the stairs, "has got the best thing of the year in his possession! Do you realize what that means, Mary? He'll spread it all over London. The damned thing will start at six to four...oh, my God! why did I come to this party?"

She saw that the situation was a serious one. Mr Frithington-Evans was in danger of losing money.

"What can we do?" she asked, for she also spelt 'life' with an £.

"He's got to be kept there until the race is over. Under no circumstances is he to be allowed to leave the house or use the telephone. You've got to put a man on to watch him day and night. As for that cursed trainer, I'll fire him as soon as the race is over. The fool, to wire!"

He conveniently forgot that he had left strict instructions that the result of the trial should be sent to his house in Berkshire.

Evans waited with growing impatience for the summons that came not. As the horror of his position gained on him, Educated Evans grew deathly pale.

Outside in the dark of Grosvenor Square two people were in earnest conversation.

"It's makin' a fool of me," said Alf Lube bitterly "bringin' me here an' keepin' me without so much as a drink – what for?"

His lady wife answered with ominous calm.

"He'll come out in a minute, oiled to the world," she said malignantly, "and if he's got information we'll get it, Alf. I'm not takin' risks – I've got two mouths to fill an' grandfather might pop off any day."

"It's makin' a fool of me," said Alf, but wisely uttered no other protest.

It was nearing midnight, and Evans was lying down on the little bed, when a step outside the door brought him to his feet.

"Are you awake?"

It was the socialistic waiter, and the hollowness of his voice through the keyhole sent a shiver down Evans' spine.

"They're goin' to do you in," said the voice pleasantly. "That burjoise that the wire was meant for, says you've got to be kept here for a week – they're goin' to starve you to death, Comrade."

"Are they – Comrade?" quavered Evans.

"The best thing you can do is to tie your sheets together and let yourself down to the street. Me and a couple of comrades will stand underneath and catch you if you fall. Long live the revolution!"

"What revolution?" asked Evans.

"Wot's coming," said the waiter, and immediately crept away.

Evans opened the window and, looking down four storeys, withdrew, dizzy. To knot three sheets together and lower yourself from a fourth-storey window is a very easy matter in books; but when there are no sheets the difficulties increase. Moreover, Evans had never knotted anything together in his life.

Another simple plan was to climb up to the roof, tap the telephone wires and call the police; but as against this, he couldn't climb, and he had never tapped anything except an old friend in his more impecunious moments.

Midnight came; one o'clock struck – two. And then, looking out of the open window, by the light of a street lamp he saw two people. They were the comrades who had come to catch him when he jumped, he guessed. Nevertheless, he did not jump.

And then a brilliant idea struck him. Pulling a paper from one pocket and a pencil from another, he wrote:

Please take this to Sergeant Challoner, the well-known Miller.

And, underneath:

Dear Mr Challoner, This comes hoping to find you quite well as I am not. Longlegs is a stone certainty for the Leigh Handicap. Would you kindly oblige by asking somebody to send this out for me to all clients, old and new?

Yours truly,
EDUCATED EVANS.

Wrapping the paper in half-a-crown, he threw it, and had the satisfaction of seeing one of the watchers pick it up…

Mr and Mrs Lube hurried home with the paper which had fallen into their hands, and a few minutes later were reading the message. When they had finished…

"A trap," said Mrs Lube. "The artful old rat! He spotted us watchin' and tried to catch us. This letter goes round to The Miller – we'll send a boy with it. Let 'em send it out! Longlegs – I'll give him Longlegs!"

Mr Lube pocketed the half-crown and felt that he was in some way repaid for his vigil.

And when, two days later, Longlegs won at 100/8, and Mr Evans was released from captivity with a ten-pound note and a warning to keep away from Grosvenor Square, there was rejoicing in Bayham Mews.

"And let me tell you, Evans," said The Miller firmly, "that's you'll get me hung if you send me letters like that. What do you think my inspector would say?"

"He'd say 'What a beauty!' Mr Challoner," said Educated Evans.

THE USER OF MEN

By some miracle, Educated Evans had recovered his prestige in Camden Town. Possibly it was the reaction from the failure of Old Sam, that ancient impostor, whose Midnight Special had napped six successive odds-on chances, only one of which succeeded in finishing in the first three.

It was significant that a certain railway Goods Yard, which is a solid body of public opinion, had turned to Evans after the remarkable victory of Longlegs at Chester, and that not only had they paid for this incomparable selection, but many of them had acted honourable afterwards. Evans had received two large Scottish salmon, with their labels obviously torn off, a bushel of apples with a label pasted over, and a small case containing three bottles of invalid wine. And then Siezem had won at Warwick at the surprising price of 100/6, and Siezem had been the Double Nap Fear Nothing Help Yourself Mid-day Special of Educated Evans.

"I got it from the boy who does him," said the exultant man of learning. "I've had that information locked up, so to speak, in my bosom for munce and munce. I've been waiting for him, I've been watching his gallops, and at last I says, 'Today's the day'."

"The story you told me last night," said the patient Miller, "was that you got so fed up with trying to find a winner that you shut your eyes and stuck it with a pin. But perhaps you're more truthful when you're sober?"

"I had two half-pints last night," said Evans reproachfully. "It's the 'eat makes me go funny like that."

Down in the little street where Old Sam had his habitation there was a great deal of heartburning, and not a little wrath. There was also a crisis. Mrs Lube was in her most vixenish mood. Not so Old Sam, who sat before the empty firegrate, his eyes closed, humming snatches of songs, the most modern of which was 'Tararaboomdeay!'

"I'm surprised at you, grandfather," said his exasperated relative. "Sitting there as drunk as a lord and not caring about me and my two poor children. Why don't you go and find things?"

"Greek Batchelor – what a beauty!" murmured Old Sam. "What a beauty, what a beauty!"

He repeated "What a beauty!" about forty times, until his voice sank to nothingness and his head followed suit. Mrs Lube looked at her husband.

"I've got forty pounds," she said deliberately.

Her husband started.

"You never have?" Then a sense of his wrongs came uppermost. "And last week I asked you to lend me – "

"I've got forty pounds, saved – from the wreck."

'She nodded at the wreck who, blissfully unconscious of this uncomplimentary reference, was sleeping noisily.

"And I've got something to do with my money besides givin' it to you to guzzle away. I'm going to take him into partnership."

"Who?" asked her lawful husband, his mind flying instantly to a certain undesirable Greek lodger.

"That Evans." The words almost choked her.

"Give him money?" Alf Lube was incredulous.

"I'm goin' to take him into partnership. He's doin' too well. That's what Mr Elmer of the Red Lion said to me: 'Why don't you go into partnership? What's the good of competition?' "

Her husband had only the vaguest idea of what constituted a partnership, and what mysterious ritual preceded its creation.

"There's no sense in scrappin' with him. What we've got to do is to make a partnership, get his addresses, make as much use of them as we can, and then – " She snapped her fingers tragically. The outlook for Educated Evans was not a promising one.

"I've not taken up with him," said the amiable Mrs Tarbet. "I'm not taking up with any man, not after my experience with George. Men! I use 'em, my dear! Come upstairs and see my new dress. I got it from Way's and it's a dream…"

On the following Saturday, The Miller was talking with the official on duty at the members' entrance at Kempton Park, when a man walked briskly past them. He wore a peaked cap around the band on which were the words Kempton Park Race Club, and he carried in his hand an important-looking blue envelope.

"Who's that bird?" asked the discreet detective.

"I don't know – one of the ground men, I expect," said the officer.

The Miller passed through the car enclosure on the heels of the messenger, followed him across the course and over the members' lawn into the paddock.

Still the man with the blue envelope walked on, until he disappeared in an outbuilding. The Miller waited. Presently the man came out, minus his envelope and wearing a crushed-looking trilby hat.

"Good morning, Evans."

Evans was momentarily startled.

"How long have you been on the staff of this race-course?" asked The Miller sternly.

For a second the educated man was embarrassed.

"It's a mild form of deception, if I may use the expression," he said, "but nobody loses nothing by it. If I didn't get into Tatt's this way I shouldn't come in at all so, in a manner of speakin', the stewards don't lose so much as a tosser. There's a horse in the first race that's money for jam. I've had him from the boy who does him. He was tried with the celebrated Golly Eyes an' walked away from him. Mugman's the name, help yourself but keep it dark."

The Miller sighed.

"Evans, I'm compounding a felony by not pinching you – my kind heart will be the ruin of me. I suppose you've got a collection of cap-bands and use a different one for each course?"

"All except Ascot," confessed Evans modestly. "It's one of the best lot of cap-bands you ever see. I call 'em my members' badges."

"What was in the envelope?"

"Nothing," said Evans shamelessly. "It's got 'To the Secretary – Urgent' on it. Nobody don't dare stop you if you've got that. It's as much as their job's worth."

Here, the representative of the law thought, was an opportune moment to deliver a lecture on morality. Evans listened meekly.

"I quite agree with you, Mr Challoner, an' I won't do it again. Honesty begins at home, as I always say, an' as the famous Lord Wolsey – him that haunts Hampton Court – said, 'If I'd only looked after myself like I've looked after other people, I shouldn't be drawin' the dole.' That's a nice-lookin' horse, Mr Challoner!"

He pointed to an animal which was being led round by a groom.

"He looks like Zionist to me – I'd recernize the horse anywhere – I seen him do a gallop up at Wantage. Funny how some people can recernize horses an' other people can't – that's Zionist all right."

"To be exact, it's the starter's hack," said The Miller patiently.

"Is that so?" Evans was respectfully interested. "It only shows, Mr Challoner, what horses come down to. As the highly respected Dr Johnstone said, 'The more 'I see of horses the more I like dogs.' That's a funny-lookin' horse goin' into the ring. I wouldn't back her with bad money. Look at her feet – look at her ribs!"

The Miller consulted his card.

"That's Mugman. Presently we shall see him fall down, get up and *then* win!" he said quietly.

Mr Evans coughed.

"Looks ain't everything," he said, very truly.

"How's business, Evans?" The Miller was kind enough to change the subject.

"Not so bad." Evans was surprisingly indifferent. "Camden Town's no good to a man like me. I'm thinkin' of takin' a office at Newmarket an' doin' things on the big scale. Advertisements everywhere – balloons over Epsom – sanwidge men with boards up an' down the West End."

"Indeed!" Mr Challoner was politely sceptical. "Have you come into a fortune?"

Evans considered this question.

"In a sense – yes," he said, and went on: "You haven't seen my young lady about, have you?"

He grew rosy under the stern eye of his companion.

"Did she have a cap-band too?" asked The Miller. "Or did she wear the cap and apron of a tea-room waitress?"

"Her?" Evans was slightly amused. "She's got money of her own – an' what a lady! Manners! You never saw manners like 'em. Talks French better than a Frenchman. Hongri, the celebrated French waiter, said that he don't understand some of the words she used. That's class. Here!" His voice sank. "I'll introduce you!"

A lady was approaching them. She was, The Miller guessed, lingering in the thirties and she was, not to put too fine a point on it, on the stout side. Without being pretty she was pleasant; the pink of her cheeks was a deep pink.

"Mrs Tarbet, permittez moi to introduce you to my friend, Mr Challoner," said Evans, who had evidently acquired the French language.

"Excuse fingers," said Mrs Tarbet briskly. "I've just been eating fish. Ain't it hot? You're here, then?" This to Evans, who smirked foolishly. "I been lookin' all over the place for you. What's goin' to win this first race? Mugman? Don't make me laugh. I've got a tip for Ooji from one of our customers. So long! I'll see you at the Assizes."

With this bright quip she passed on.

"She's never, so to speak, at a loss for an answer," said the admiring Evans. "Witty? She'd make a cat laugh!"

"Barmaid?" asked The Miller, who was not easily amused.

"She owns property," said Evans impressively: "two public-houses an' a block of flats!"

"And you come into the last category," said The Miller, who occasionally employed words which were more Greek than French to Educated Evans.

A few minutes later he joined the lady in the sealskin coat.

"Who was that bird you introduced me to, Evans?" she asked, a little resentfully. "Don't go introducin' me to your race-course friends, I beg."

"He's one of the stewards," exaggerated Evans, and the lady was mollified.

They had met at the cinema; she had trodden on his toe by accident – for she was ladylike and would not descend to a vulgar subterfuge – and at his invitation they had supped together at Isaacs' Fish Bar. She was a widow and lonely. She admired cleverness and education. Mr Evans had the goods. He was both clever and educated. At Isaacs' Fish Bar she learned for the first time that the world went round the sun once in twenty-four hours, that people used to be hanged at Marble Arch, and that Ormonde won the Derby in a snow-storm and had to have butter put on his feet to help him slip round Tattenham Corner. She was also instructed in mediaeval history, and discovered that B – Mary, Queen of Scotch, was not all that a lady should be, and that Julius Caesar, the far-famed Italian, signed the Magna Charter and laid the foundations of the Rules of Racing.

Nevertheless, being a monied woman, she was not willing to submit her intelligence to the domination of any man, however learned.

"Come along and see this race, and we'll have a chat afterwards about The Business. I don't want to put my money into anything that I can't see my way out of."

The moral position of Educated Evans was strengthened when Mugman scrambled home a head in front of the horse he had backed. Even Mrs Lucy Tarbet was impressed.

"Logic an' deduction an' information v. guesswork," murmured Evans, surreptitiously tearing up the ticket which, if the second had won, would have brought him five very necessary pounds. "That horse was sent out to three thousand clients…" Then, remembering that she would certainly want to see his books, "or, rather, would have been sent out, only I was in such a hurry to meet you that I only had time to send thirty wires. If I had a bit of capital…"

He enlarged upon the prospects. Mrs Tarbet listened thoughtfully.

"How much do you want?" she asked.

Evans dared not say, in case he put the figure too low.

"Thousands," he suggested.

"Fiddlesticks!" said Mrs Tarbet, scornfully. "I wouldn't mind putting fifty pounds into it."

"Fifty!" he laughed hollowly. "Why, fifty pounds wouldn't go nowhere!"

She nibbled the end of her glove, frowning.

"Do you know any other horse that's going to win today?" she asked.

Evans smiled.

"Brass Nail is a stone certainty," he said. "The common people will back Blue Nose. An' in the last race High Up can't be beat. I got him from a girl who's got a sister who walks out with the head lad."

"I'll tell you what I'll do," said Mrs Tarbet. "Just wait here."

She hurried into the ring and came back with a smile of triumph.

"I said I'd put fifty pounds into your business. Well, I've put it on to your horse! We'll see what happens. I've got ten to one with my friend Mr Izzy Friedman."

Evans looked at her wildly.

"What do you want to waste money like that for?" he blurted.

"Waste?" Mrs Tarbet's eyebrows went up.

"Well, not exactly waste," said the palpitating Evans. "But putting all that money on...it ain't much, but it might do a bit of advertising."

"Don't let's discuss it," she said coldly.

He followed her, a miserable man, back to the ring. His misery was not long-lived. Brass Nail made all the running and won by a neck.

"Well, perhaps you're right after all," he beamed. "Five hundred and fifty – you can do a lot with five hundred and fifty."

"Ye-es," said Mrs Tarbet thoughtfully. "Tell me that bit about High Up again."

"You're not going to back another horse?" said Evans, in alarm. "With five hundred and fifty we could do some advertising – "

She made an impatient noise.

"Don't let's talk business, please Mr Evans," she said, and he was crushed to silence.

Just before the last race, she found him leaning miserably over the rails of the saddling ring.

"I've just seen a friend of mine, and he says that High Up hasn't got any chance at all."

"I don't care nothing about what he says," said the wretched Evans. "If you're going to back horses, back 'em! If you're going to tip horses, tip 'em! You can't mix it. I've tried. What I say is this: put two hundred pounds into advertisin', put two hundred pounds into a office; put a hundred into expenses, keep fifty for yourself…"

But he was addressing the air. Mrs Tarbet was making her rapid way back to Tattersall's.

He roused himself sufficiently to stroll into the ring, climb to the top of the littered stand, and watch a race which had no more interest for him than the golden dome of the steward's stand. He didn't even know the colours of High Up, and until he saw the number in the frame and consulted his card, he was not aware that High Up had won. And then, with a wildly beating heart, he dashed down into the ring.

"What price was that?" he asked, almost incoherently.

"Four to one," somebody told him, and he flew through Tattersall's into the paddock, searching vainly for his inamorata.

She was standing talking to a number of obese friends when he flew up to her, his face beaming.

"You was right after all, Lucy," he said.

She transfixed him with an icy stare: obviously she was in a very bad temper.

"Mrs Tarbet, if you please," she snapped. "Please go away. I don't want to hear any more about your beastly horses. If you don't go, I'll call a policeman!"

Evans reeled back, pallid of face, as these words fell from the fresh red lips of the User of Men. He tried to speak, but she silenced him with a gesture, and dejectedly he slouched across the paddock, his hands in his pockets, the picture of misery.

He was wandering towards the open horse gate, and as he was half-way between the unsaddling ring and the gate, the horses were coming. And between the jockeys on the first two there was something like unpleasantness. Evans heard…

"you bored me out from the rails, you dirty dog… Of course I'm going to object…"

An objection! Evans was electrified. This fat vampire had friends in the ring. At the word 'Objection' she would fly to one of her bookmaking pals and save her money. Hell hath no fury like a turf prophet scorned. He would be avenged on this woman. Instantly, as the idea took shape, he turned and ran across the paddock. Mrs Tarbet was still talking to one of her friends, and at the sight of the dishevelled Evans her face clouded.

"Excuse me, Mrs Tarbet, for one minute. I've something very important to say to you," he begged urgently. "It's not about business, it's about somethin' that goin' to happen next week…"

"Excuse me," she said frigidly to her friend, and consented to walk with Evans out of earshot.

What wild story he told her, he never remembered. It was evidently something fascinating, for she listened open-mouthed, her attention so concentrated that she never heard the cry of 'Objection.'

There was no need for her to go into the ring. She had arranged for her money to be sent to her by cheque. After about five minutes…

"I don't know what on earth you're talking about, Evans," she said raucously. "You're simply wasting my time with a lot of nonsense about a horse that'll run on Wednesday. I don't want any more of your tips, and I don't want any more to do with you. You're simply coming after my money, and I can't stand spongers."

Evans could swallow the insult and smile. He must keep her engaged in conversation so that there was no possibility of her saving her money. The red flag was flying, but this Mrs Tarbet did not notice. And then a blessed word reached him. Somebody shouted "Sustained!" and the faint sound of it came to his ears. At that moment Evans was magnificent.

"Thank you very kindly for your attention, Mrs Tarbet, and I can only say, in conclusion that, having done in your stuff, we'll cry quits."

"What do you mean – 'done in my stuff,' you guttersnipe?" she asked angrily.

"Your horse is disqualified," he hissed. "Rat's Tail has got the race on an objection!"

"High Up disqualified!" she shrieked. "My Gawd! I backed Rat's Tail!"

THE LADY WATCH DOG

Satan, the original labour exchange for Idle Hands, put it into the heart of Alf Lube that the diamond-encircled wrist-watch worn by Mrs Arabella Fich, the proprietress of the Three Dogs public-house in Stibbington Street, could do him a bit of good. Mrs Fich was an absent-minded woman and had the habit, when she assisted in the bar, of putting her watch on a little shelf at the back of the bar. A man – said the Evil One – with a long reach and a walking-stick, could hook out that watch without the slightest exertion.

One Thursday evening, when trade was very bad, Mr Lube turned into the saloon bar and found its other occupant, a solitary man sitting on a high stool and thoughtfully regarding a glass of whisky and water. Mr Lube's lip curled.

"Hullo, Evans," he said coarsely. "Been welshing lately?"

Educated Evans regarded him with the look of a wounded fawn.

"Politeness costs nothing," he said mildly.

"Been down to Epsom lately?"

Evans did not reply.

"I wonder a man like you's got the nerve to show himself in a bar parlour," nagged Alf. "Here, missis, give me a small bitter. I can't afford whisky – I don't welsh."

"Nor work," said Evans, still regarding his glass.

Mr Lube's chubby face darkened.

"I don't welsh," he said.

"Nor work," said Evans absently; "not since you come out of stir, anyway."

It was true that on three occasions Mr Lube had been put away for trifling offences. But to be told by a man like Evans…

"You're askin' for it!" he said, breathing through his nose. "I've killed men for less than that!"

Evans lifted his glass, smelt the contents and drank leisurely.

"You're an uneducated man," he said, after the last gurgle, "and if Old Sam wasn't keepin' you, you'd be in Pentonville. As for your wife – "

"Don't say a word against my wife!" hissed Mr Lube, making a fear-inspiring face and edging closer.

"I'm sorry for you, Lube," said Evans, getting down from his stool. "You can't help your misfortune. Buy yourself a drink."

He put down half a crown on the counter and walked out. Lube glared after him, pouched the half crown and drank his bitter bitterly.

He was not a fighting man. And Evans had spoken the truth. The Lube family was at the point of crisis. That very night his wife had refused him a shilling, though she knew that his unemployment pay was due on the morrow. Moreover, she had refused him the wherewithal to go to Kempton.

His eyes, roving the bar, rested on the sparkling watch half hidden from view between two claret glasses. He knew a fence at Finsbury who would give him at least a fiver for that. Mr Lube hesitated. It was so long since he had broken the law that he had almost acquired the habit of honesty. The four ale bar was empty; the barmaid was at the other end of the bar, her back towards him, engrossed in a book.

He lifted his walking-stick tentatively, laid it on the counter, stretched… The watch dropped in his pocket. In a few seconds he was in the street.

"What's the matter with you, Alf?"

Mrs Lube was engaged in preparing a rough balance sheet of Old Sam's Midnight Special when her husband came in. One glance at his face told her everything, for his was an easy face to read.

"Nothin'." He was very jerky of speech. "Thought I'd go up an' see a friend of mine at Finsbury – "

She held out her large hand.

"Drop." she said tersely.

Alf spluttered, bullied, lied, but in the end the watch was lying in her palm.

"Mrs Fich's," she said calmly. "You're a nice father of a family, I don't think!"

He tried to bluster his way out. By accident he touched the right note.

"It's that 'ound Evans – he got me wild, the way he talked about you an' – an' the lodger. He said no wonder we tipped Greek Batchelor…"

Mr Dimitri, the good-looking Greek lodger, had departed from the home of the Lubes after a terrific scene. Alf felt he might put into Mr Evans' mouth some of the private thoughts on the subject which he had not hitherto dared to express on his own behalf.

"Oh, he did, did he?" said Mrs Lube, grey with fury. "An' you sat round an' said nothing! A dam' fine husband you are!"

One lie was as easy as another. Alf described how he had caught the traducer by the throat and shaken him sick. His wife did not believe him but was appeased. She looked at the watch again.

"He was in the bar when you went in?" she asked. "Now you go up to bed and keep your big mouth shut, or I'll take the rollin' pin to you like I did last Good Friday!"

Alf meekly obeyed.

Mrs Lube decided to make a call on Educated Evans next day, and she did so at a moment when the World's Champion Prophet and Turf Adviser was engaged in the case of Henrietta Bowsome.

Educated Evans had never heard of Henrietta Bowsome, and might never have heard of her, for he seldom read anything else in a newspaper than the columns in which racing correspondents explain why their selections did not win the day before; but it happened that he was in attendance at the police court, a client of his having fallen into grievous error.

Educated Evans, because of his erudition and his well-known gifts in the matter of terminology, had prepared the defence which was read from the dock and instantly recognized.

"I think," said The Miller *sotto voce* to his protegé as they walked out into the lobby, "that if it hadn't been for that defence of yours, young Herbert would have got off. As it is, he's going to do three months. Why don't you change your style?"

Evans raised his eyebrows and said nothing. It was useless to argue with Detective-Sergeant Challoner in his more aggravating mood.

"Is Henrietta a client of yours, by the way?" asked The Miller.

"Henrietta? I don't know the gentleman."

"It's a lady, to be exact," said The Miller, and described Henrietta's weakness.

She was a shopper. It was her custom to walk into one of those crowded departmental stores which ornament Oxford Street, carrying on her hands a large muff. A muff is a very convenient appendage to a lady with a weakness for acquiring property in the Homeric manner, for what Henrietta

> ...thought she might require
> She went and took.

Interested, Evans strolled back to the court, in time to see a very pretty, well-dressed girl step blithely into the dock, nod smilingly to the unresponsive magistrate, and glance round the court with the air of one who is visiting her old home and is gratified to discover that nothing had been changed. And at the end of the evidence...

"Really, Henrietta, I don't know what to do with you," said the magistrate, leaning back in his chair and taking off his glasses. "You are incorrigible!"

"It's very difficult for me to find work with my record," said Henrietta. She had a soft, cooing, almost pathetic voice.

The magistrate shook his head.

"The probation officer can do nothing with you. This thieving – "

"Kleptomania," murmured Henrietta. "It runs in the family. My father was a tax-collector."

The magistrate gazed sternly round the court.

"I will not have any laughing in this court," he said. "This is a very serious matter, and unless you can find somebody who is willing to employ you and be guarantee for your good behaviour, I shall have to send you to prison."

He waited expectantly.

"I will," said Evans huskily.

He had had no more intention of intervening in this case than he had of kissing a policeman.

The magistrate put on his glasses again, the better to observe the philanthropist.

"Oh, you're Evans, aren't you?"

"Yes, my lord," said the educated man.

"Is he a householder?"

The Miller came to the rescue here, inwardly cursing his friend, and confessed that Evans was indeed, a householder.

"But what on earth can you do with this girl? Are you an employer of labour?"

Evans nodded dumbly. In justice to him, although he was acting on impulse, he was prompted by the subconscious knowledge that he needed assistance in the great and beneficent work of conveying to the sporting public information which even owners and trainers did not possess. For Evans had had the good fortune to tip a 20/1 winner at Sandown Park.

The magistrate heaved a deep, dissatisfied sigh.

"All right; she'll be bound over in the sum of twenty pounds on your recognizances, Mr Evans." And his tone suggested that he would have added: "And I wish you joy of your bargain," but he was a kind-hearted man and did not wish to depress unduly one who had undertaken a task of such magnitude.

"You've done it, my lad," said The Miller under his breath. "This is going to cost you twenty of the best and brightest! She'll be up again before the old man within a week."

Evans was too interested in his new responsibility to heed the warning.

She was a pretty girl, this Henrietta, in a pinkish way, with a trick of showing her white teeth, for she was easily amused. For the moment she was a little scared, too, for she had served one period as a guest of the proprietors of Holloway Castle, and she had no desire to repeat her experience.

"I don't know what makes me do it, Mr Evans," she said, as they walked towards Bayham Mews together. "But somehow, when I see loose property laying around, I've got to hook it or die."

"You listen to me, Henrietta," said Evans soberly, and in the manner of a father, "and you'll not go far wrong. Come to me for advice. If you find the temptation a-overcomin' you, out of business hours, just pop round and see me."

She looked at him in surprise.

"But I shan't have to pop round, shall I?" she asked. "Aren't you going to give me some work?"

"There's plenty of work," said Evans enthusiastically, "and what's more, you'll be well paid for it. Can you typewrite?"

She said she thought she could.

"It would teach me to spell," she said. Later he discovered how bad a speller she was.

"You stick to me, Henrietta," he said, in his best parental manner; "never say a word of what goes on inside my office, be my watch dog, and you'll Make Money. I'll show you the office."

The office had an occupant. Mrs Lube in her best clothes and wearing all the family jewels, was sitting in the one chair, fanning herself with the afternoon paper. Her manner was gracious; she even smiled, though the smile vanished and a look of surprise and understanding came into her bulgeous eyes when the girl followed Evans into the room.

"Good morning, Mr Evans," she said sweetly.

Evans left the door wide open and stood at a respectful distance.

"My dear grandfather sent me round to ask if you'd be good enough to tell him what you're sending out for the Chester Cup," she said, almost apologetically. "He says he wouldn't like to send the same horse because people might talk."

Evans was thunderstruck. This advance from the enemy's camp was amazing. He could hardly believe his ears.

"Eh...well, Mrs Lube...to tell you the truth, I was thinkin' of sendin' Laberens."

Again Mrs Lube smiled.

"It's so good of you, Mr Evans," she said, as she rose to go. "Perhaps you'll slip round an' have a sociable drink one day?"

She was gone before he recovered from the shock.

"Me have a drink with her!" he said at last. "Would I take a sitlitz powder from the hands of the celebrated Lewd-creature Burgia, the female Crippen of Rome, Italy?"

"Who is she?" asked Miss Bowsome curiously.

"She's Nothing," said Evans, and changed the subject. "This is my little den," he explained. "I've thought out some of the best winners here that any man's ever found. In that there corner by the fireplace I got the idea for Braxted – 20/ 1, what a beauty! – on that table I writ or wrote Taping – Fear Nothing; I lay on that bed an' thought out Paddy – 20/ 1, what a beauty...!"

Henrietta looked round the historic apartment without any visible signs of enthusiasm.

"Where's the other room?" she asked.

"What other room?" demanded Evans.

"Where do *I* sleep?" she demanded, her innocent eyes on his.

Evans stared at her.

"Ain't you got a home?" he asked.

"Of course I haven't got a home." she replied scornfully. "What's more, I can't get lodgings. I've got such a bad name that nobody will trust me in Camden Town,"

The colour left the cheeks of the World's Greatest Tipster.

"You can't stay here," he squeaked. "This is *my* room!"

She sat down in the one chair and folded her arms.

"I've got to stay here," she said steadily. "You're in charge of me: the magistrate said so. Besides, how can I keep honest if I'm away from you? The moment I get out of your sight I shall be pinching something; I can't help it, Mr Evans!"

Educated Evans took half a cigar from the mantelshelf with a hand that shook, and lit it unsteadily.

"This is a nice thing!" he said, in a tone which meant that it was anything but that. "I've got myself into a nice kind of trouble through helping young women, I must say!"

"Haven't you got any place where you can sleep?" she asked innocently. "Couldn't you take lodgings?"

Evans grew testy.

"I can't have you sleeping here, getting me a bad name," he said, with vigour and vehemence. "It's ridiculous an' absurd. Why, I'll have people pointing the finger of scorn at me, as though I was one of them celebrated pashers of Hindustan."

Her eyes lit up.

"With divans and things," she breathed, "and beautiful Indian curtains and wonderful Persian rugs on the floor! Like in films!"

Evans was staggered.

"I'm not a pasher, and I never will be a pasher," he said sternly. "Nobody's ever breathed the breath of scandal against me. I'm like Caesar's celebrated friend, Cleopatra, whose well-known needle we all admire – see Shakespeare – "

"Couldn't you sleep out somewhere?" she interrupted his discourse to ask. "It's so easy for you, Mr Evans."

Her voice had in it that note of pathos which so touched him.

"I'm a poor girl – lonely and friendless, with everybody's hand against me, Mr Evans. I'm not educated like you are, Mr Evans. I know I shan't be reformed – I've tried to be. But give me a chance, Mr Evans. If I could only raise enough money to get to Canada, I might marry a farmer and live in the country where there's nothing to pinch but corn."

The upshot of it was that Evans took a room with his friend, the van driver. It was not an arrangement exactly pleasing to him, as he told The Miller that night when they met in the High Street outside the cinema.

"You're a fool," said The Miller. "And what's more, you're going to get a bad name. That girl can't help stealing. Her parents were that way. She can hardly write her own name and her general education is nil!"

"She's fond of poetry – she told me so," said Henrietta's defender, stoutly.

"Pah!" snarled The Miller. "Poetry!"

Early the next morning, as he was strolling to the station, he was intercepted by Mrs Lube, who had heard, it seems, the plaintive outcry of the landlady of the Three Dogs and had certain information to impart...

At that moment, when The Miller and the voluble Mrs Lube sat in the inspector's room, Evans entered Bayham Mews, determined to regularize an intolerable situation. The van-driver's bed was hard. Mr Evans could not bring his mind to the contemplation of the thoroughbred race-horse in an alien atmosphere. Henrietta must find lodgings. He had practically arranged this.

But when he got to his office the girl was not there.

The bed was neatly made; the floor was brushed; the hearth tidied; but Henrietta had vanished.

On the table was a note.

Dear Mr Evins. – Fairwell. Try to forgit me. The ruleing pasions are very strong. If you carnt go write you must go rong.

Yours truely,
HENRIETTA.

P.S. – Excuse speling the potry was on a sell door at Holloway.

Evans breathed a sigh of relief. For the moment he thought nothing of the possible estreatment of his recognizances.

He had taken up his pen to indite a frenzied appeal to the speculative classes, when he heard men coming up the stairs. The Miller came in first, and behind him was a man whom Evans recognized as a detective-constable.

"Sorry to disturb you, Evans," said The Miller. "You were in the Three Dogs the other night?"

Evans was shaking.

"Yes, Mr Challoner," he said.

"While you were there, Mrs Fich lost a wrist-watch the value of which is over £250. It was stolen from a shelf behind the bar. There is information that you left the bar hurriedly, and I have a warrant to search your room."

Educated Evans said not a word, but stood like a man in a dream, watching the systematic combing of his room.

"Nothing here," said The Miller; "not that I expected to find anything."

He lit a cigarette and, as he did so asked carelessly:

"Mrs Lube been in your room lately?"

"Yesterday," said Evans. "I found her here when I got back from the court."

The Miller smiled grimly.

"Where's Henrietta?" he asked.

"Gorn," said Evans, and showed him the letter.

The Miller read it carefully.

"You found a winner when you took that girl," he said.

When he left Zionist House, he went straight back to Mrs Lube's home.

"Thank you for the information, Mrs Lube," he said dryly; "and I'll tell you straight away that when your husband says that he saw Evans reaching with a stick, I don't believe him."

"Did you find the watch, Mr Challoner?" she asked anxiously. "An' did you pinch the thievin' hound?"

"I didn't find the watch," said The Miller carefully, "and Evans didn't find it."

"Did you look under the mattress?" asked the agitated woman. "That's where thieves hide property."

"And that's where they find it too," said The Miller cryptically.

THE JOURNALIST

Mr Frithington-Evans had a colt, Sunsweet, by Sunstar out of Toffee. It was trained by an old stud groom who knew more about horses than most trainers. From time to time Mr Frithington-Evans sent a good handicapper to Shropshire to try this wonderful two-year-old, and every trial aroused joy in the shrivelled soul of this rich young man, who was a sportman by profession and a gentleman by custom.

It was arranged that the horse should be brought to Alexandra Park, where the opposition was unimportant, and by skilful organization, Mr Frithington-Evans secured one thousand seven hundred and fifty-two bookmakers' accounts. Some were in his own name, some in fictitious names. In defiance of the laws of racing he advertised through a trusty agent and in this way obtained accounts to reach the total given. On the day of the race the wires would be sent from a hundred sub-post offices in London, each batch being preceded by long-winded telegrams addressed to himself, the idea being to delay the despatch of the wires. It was what Educated Evans called a 'coop.' Unfortunately…

Mr Frithington-Evans was by nature and inclination a twister. He twisted Lord Bascom – Viscount Bascom of Bascom – to the extent of fifteen hundred pounds. Not that Frithy needed the money. He had so much that he was ill with it, but it was his nature to twist.

Lord Bascom was very annoyed, and with good reason when, at their club, Frithy coolly denied that he had ever promised to put a monkey on Longlegs for his friend the first time he was trying.

"Imagination, dear old boy," he said coolly. "You're dreaming!"

Now, although Lord Bascom was an extremely wealthy man – he was chairman of fourteen companies – he was also an extremely mean man. And he hated losing fifteen hundred pounds.

"You're a dirty skunk," he roared, "and one of these days I'm going to get even with you!"

Mr Frithington-Evans grinned, and that grin cost him a lot of money.

"You blabbed Longlegs all over the place – and I got three to one to my money," he said.

His lordship did not call him a simple liar. He added something.

"Didn't you kidnap a dirty tipster, and didn't he manage to get the news out of the house that Longlegs was a certainty? Why the man didn't bring an action against you for illegal imprisonment, I don't know. You've caught me, Frithy, and I shall catch you or my name's not Bascom!"

"Good luck!" said Frithy cheerfully, having no fears.

Lord Bascom went back to his office, red in the neck and breathing vengeance stertorously. It had been on the tip of his tongue to talk about a certain horse called Sunsweet – for his lordship lived in Shropshire, near the secret training quarters, and the best of servants talk. And then by chance there fell into his hands a copy of an unique publication...

There was no greater admirer, nor more consistent supporter, of Educated Evans, than Mr Bert Sybil, the printer. He did everything for Evans except lend him money; and in justice to our friend, such a request never came from the World's Champion Prophet and Turf Adviser. He had even expressed a willingness to print Mr Evans' tips at cost price but, as Educated Evans pointed out to him, the inspiration for his selections came so late in the day that it would be a waste of money to put them into cold type.

Evans was working late one night, revising his tattered list of clients, when Mr Sybil called upon him, and the visit was a little surprising, because Evans believed that Mr Sybil was a wealthy man who could well afford the services of a professional mouthpiece. As it happened, he did not come in search of advocacy.

"Heard about my trouble, Evans?"

"Yes, Mr Sybil. Sit down, won't you?"

Evans himself sat on the table, placing the only chair in the room at the disposal of his visitor. Mr Sybil sighed.

"I'm afraid I'm for it this time," he said. "Trade's bad, or I wouldn't have taken on the job. You're a man of the world and you understand that."

Evans understood and sympathized. For the third time in three years Mr Sybil had been summoned by the police for printing the tickets of an illicit sweepstake. He had been fined large sums, and had had ominous warnings.

"I'm afraid they're going to put me away this time, Evans," said Mr Sybil, gazing reflectively at his cigar. "I've been in before, but nobody knows that but you and me. I tried to straighten The Miller, but he wouldn't be squared. Now the point is, what's going to happen to the business when I'm away. I've got a sort of manager, but I don't trust him any farther than I can chuck him. I'm not married, I've got no relations, and there's nobody in Camden Town that I can put in charge. Do you know anything about printing?"

Evans' first inclination was to give a history of the printing art from its inception by the celebrated Klaxon in 1066, but on reflection he decided to deny all knowledge of the trade.

Mr Sybil smoked thoughtfully for a long time without speaking.

"You know enough about it to pay the wages bill, I suppose? I've got a dozen contracts that'll keep the works going till I come out. What I want is somebody to keep an eye on it as if it was his own. I don't mind paying four or five pounds a week," he added.

Although Educated Evans knew nothing about printing, he knew a great deal about four or five pounds a week, and after two hours spent in instructions and warnings, the arrangements were made, and Mr Sybil's foresight was justified when, on the following morning, he was sent to prison for two months.

"It's a bit hard on me," complained Evans to his chief confidant. "What with the rush of business and the lies that Old Sam and his granddaughter's tellin' about me, an' Ascot comin' on, I haven't got any time to mess about with printing businesses. I've got all my work cut out gettin' lists."

Addresses are the life-blood of the tipster. There are many eminent firms of publishers which issue classified dictionaries of various trades. You may discover at a glance all the ironmongers and most of the linen-drapers who do business in England. You may, by the turning of a page, have revealed to your eyes the directors of public companies. But up to date, nobody had published a volume indispensable to every turf prophet – a Dictionary of Mugs.

There goes on a trade in addresses which is a lucrative one. One tipster, having exhausted his credit and the patience of his clients, will sell his list to another of his profession who, employing a new method of approach and a new appeal to the credulity of his clients, may revive in their bosoms the hope and faith which are so essential to the well-being of the turf prophet.

"If I can only get a list or two, Mr Challoner, I'll be playing banker at the well-known Monte Carlo."

Now The Miller, like most officers of the Criminal Investigation Department, had an extensive knowledge of the odd trades of London; and the list-touter was a familiar object on his mental landscape. And he knew that these evil men sometimes produced lists which had been assiduously copied from reputable directories, and were of no more value to a hardworking turf prophet than a copy of the *War Cry* would be to a system worker.

"Who's offering you a list?" he asked and, after a second's hesitation – for Evans had a natural objection to supplying information to the police:

"Joe Liski," he said, and The Miller smiled.

"Joe couldn't fall straight if he fell out of a balloon," he said picturesquely. "Take my advice, Evans: let Mrs Lube buy all the lists she wants, and you stick to your own. Why don't you advertise?"

Mr Evans closed his eyes.

"As the celebrated Queen Elizabeth said to Cardinal Rishloo, when he asked her why she didn't get married: 'Ask me another.'

Them newspapers are too particular, and they're very expensive, Mr Challoner, and they want to know all your private affairs – "

"Such as whether the winner you say you sent out, you actually did send?" suggested The Miller and, as Evans evaded the question, he was probably right. "Why not start a newspaper of your own? You've got the business."

The idea only then dawned upon Educated Evans.

"A paper?" he said thoughtfully. "Bless my soul! Evans' Weekly, or the Educated Magazine!"

As soon as he could, with politeness, shake himself clear of The Miller's company, he hurried to the little side street where Sybil's Printing Works were situated. The foreman and manager, a thin, shifty man, was surprisingly helpful.

"You could do it for about twelve pounds a week," he said, after making rough calculations on the back of a bill. "You want a boy on a bicycle to take the papers round to the shops – what are you going to charge for it?"

"Five bob?" suggested Evans.

The printer took a pinch of snuff – printers who do not take snuff have no right to their title.

"What about sixpence?" he said, brutally, and added: "I don't mind doing this job: it'll liven things up a bit. It hasn't been the same place since the governor's been away. We never had a week pass that the police didn't come in, and that stopped you feeling dull."

The scheme now took definite shape, and Evans applied himself to his new avocation with tremendous intensity.

The magic of printers' ink was in his blood. For three days he neglected all business, while he moved deliriously through the grime and ruin of a jobbing printer's office. For there is this about all such places: that they have the appearance of having survived a bad earthquake which was accompanied by a phenomenal shower of soot.

The news came to the Old Sam faction in the nature of a shock.

" 'Im with a paper!" said Mrs Lube, aghast at the suggestion. "I'll believe it when I see it."

She saw it soon enough. The first number of *Evans' Imperial Racing Guide and Backer's Friend* appeared on the Tuesday. It consisted of four very small pages, but there was meat and drink in every line. One column was headed:

WHAT I SAW WITH MY OWN EYES.

By Educated Evans, the World's Premier Profit and Turf Adviser

Down at Kempton the other day I had a good look at Fluky Jane. She wasn't trying a yard. Where were the stewards?

How long will it be before Mr Frithington-Evans, the celebrated owner of Longlegs, is warned off? This man is a curse to the turf, besides being a low-spirited hound.

I understand that a great coop is intended with Mugman. This horse won at Hurst Park when I tipped it. What a beauty! What a beauty! But his trainer ought to be warned off for the way he ran at Sandown.

Mr Challoner, the celebrated detective officer, who is highly respected by Camden Town, as all the world knows, has his eye upon a certain beer-eater who calls himself a turf profit. If this man had his rights he would be doing time.

Styme, the foreman, read these notes with great relish.

"They're a bit personal, ain't they, Mr Evans?"

"They've, got to be," said Evans, who had sat up all night in the printing office in order to get the first copy of the paper. "I'm goin' to clean the turf. Many a horse sent out by me has had his head pulled off as soon as it was known that Educated Evans had give 'im!"

Mr Stym scratched his chin thoughtfully.

"Well, the old man's inside and he can't see it," he said with satisfaction. "But didn't there ought to be some tips in the paper?"

Evans gasped. He had forgotten the tips!

Mrs Lube read the paper from title to imprint. It was not the reference to her sacred grandparent that really annoyed her, so much as certain paragraphs marked

PERSONAL CHIT-CHAT AND CAMDEN TOWN GOSSIP

(by Educated Evans, the World's Champion Profit and Turf Adviser).

The goings on of the lower classes is getting worse and worse. The Greek Batchelor having been kicked out of its lodgings, still meets the fair English lady at the cinema, as I have seen with my own eyes…

Mrs Lube choked, went purple, crushed the paper in her hand and flung it into the grate; thought better of it and smoothed it out; then she grabbed her hat, and pulled it viciously over her head. She dashed into the kitchen, selected a small but heavy rolling-pin, put it in the shopping bag and went out in search of Evans.

Evans saw her coming; barricaded the door, and conducted his negotiations through the window, keeping well out of sight and out of reach.

"You dirty, slanderous, perjurous 'ound!" screamed the enraged female. "Open that door to me and I'll…" She enumerated the various portions of his anatomy on which, given the opportunity, she would experiment.

"Go away before I send for the police," shouted Evans.

"I'll 'police' you, you perjurous…"

She had a large supply of adjectives, and Evans, listening, realized that journalism had its drawbacks and its dangers.

Happily for him, Evans' *Imperial Racing Guide and Backer's Friend* enjoyed a strictly local circulation, and other gentlemen who might have had just cause for resentment at his exposure of their weaknesses were blissfully ignorant of the charges which he brought against them.

When Mr Evans got home that night he found a man sitting on the bottom step of the wooden stairs which led to his room. At first anticipating violence, he put himself in an attitude of defence.

"That you, Evans?" growled a voice. "What the devil do you mean by keeping me waiting here? I told you I should come at ten o'clock."

"Me, sir?" said Evans. "Nobody told me nothin'. Come upstairs."

He recognized, by the acerbity and haughtiness of his caller, that he had a gentleman to deal with. The mystery was explained partially when he found a letter which had evidently been pushed under his door. The visitor also found an explanation, for he snatched the letter from Evans' hand.

"I want to talk to you, and I can only spare five minutes. Are you the owner of this rubbish?"

He produced a carefully folded copy of *Evans' Imperial Racing Guide and Backer's Friend*.

"I'm the owner and I'm not the owner," said Evans, temporizing. "All the nasty things in that paper was written by a friend of mine – "

"Never mind who wrote it. A lot of it's true. You know Frithington-Evans, don't you? Of course, you're the fellow that he locked up in his room. Why the devil didn't you sue him?"

"Could I?" said Evans, with a new interest in life.

"Of course you could, you fool!" said his lordship. "You could have got a couple of thousand pounds out of the little so-and-so! Now I want you to do something for me. When does your paper come out?"

"Any day," said Evans, recklessly disregarding the regular habits of well-conducted weekly newspapers.

"I'll tell you something. I'm going to spoil Frithy's little joke. He's no relation of yours?"

"No, thank Gawd!" said Evans, and his pious denial aroused the first sign of pleasure that the visitor had displayed.

"Well, now, listen. Get out a new paper, and put in a paragraph something like this: 'Sunsweet will win at Alexandra Park.' Send it out to all your friends – the more the better – and there you are. Now how much will it cost?" He took out a pocket-book.

Evans wasn't quite certain whether to say £2 or £5.

"Will a hundred do?"

Evans, speechless, nodded.

"Now how many people can you send this out to?"

Evans thought.

"About two thousand," he suggested,

"Humph!" said his lordship. And then an idea struck him. "Come to my office in the morning, or rather, to the office of a friend of mine, and I'll give you a list of people to whom you can send this paper. But mind you, you've got to keep in the paragraph about that scoundrel being warned off! If you can think of anything worse to say, don't hesitate to say it. Here is the address: if I'm not there – of course I shan't be there," he added hastily, "because it's not my office – ask for the secretary."

He wrote down the address on the blotting-pad and left without further ceremony. All that evening he sat up, till two o'clock in the morning, compiling a list of people to whom the reference to Mr Frithington-Evans, and particularly the reference to Sunsweet, would bring joy and profit. It was not a long list, about two hundred in all.

At three o'clock the next afternoon, Mr Evans, having made the necessary alterations in his paper, came into Basinghall Street, passed the imposing portal, and knocked at the door of the room to which he had been directed. A harassed secretary appeared.

"Lists?" said the lady with a frown. "Oh, yes, you're the man Lord Bascom was expecting."

She went to a telephone and Evans heard her.

"Man come for the list…yes, my lord, Evans…on your desk? You don't mean…all right, my lord!" The latter rather hastily.

Lord Bascom! Evans knew the name, and remembered dimly having had the nobleman pointed out to him on a race-course. So he was under the distinguished patronage of Lord Bascom! He glowed.

Presently the secretary returned with a large roll of paper.

"Bring this list back when you've finished with it," she said.

It was an enormous list: it contained nearly five thousand names, and Evans had to recruit all sorts of odd labour to prepare the wrappers. He spent the greater part of the night superintending the new edition. All unnecessary paragraphs, save that relating to Mr Frithington-Evans, were deleted, and, in large letters:

Under the patronage of his lordship, Lord Bascom, Educated Evans, the Wizard of Camden Town! The World's Premier Profit and Turf Adviser; Braxted – what a beauty!

His lordship has give me a tip which same will be sent for 10/- P.O. addressed to H Evans, Greek Batchelor House, Bayham Mews. This is a beauty! It can't be beat! Given to me by one of the world's grandest old sportsmen, God bless him!…

Evans was too much of a professional to send out Sunsweet or any other sweet without making sure that he got something out of it.

Lord Bascom had been called away into the country, so he never saw, until it was too late, the unauthorized use of his name. Had he known that the document supplied to the wretched tipster was a list of the shareholders of his company, he would have died on the spot.

Old Sam and his coterie read the come on and wondered how long it would be before Evans was putting out his tin at Dartmoor.

"It's forgery, that's what it is," said Alf. "It stands to reason that no gentleman's going to have anythin' to do with a tyke like that…"

The Miller saw the paragraph and was really alarmed. He hastened round to Bayham Mews and found Mr Evans entirely surrounded by telegraph envelopes, and huge stacks of postal orders piled up on the table.

"It's rolling in – Sunsweet, help yourself," said the exuberant tipster. "Twelve hundred and forty-two pounds ten up to date, Miller!" He was hysterical with joy. "They're comin' in faster than I can open 'em!"

"Did he give you this tip?" asked The Miller.

"He certainly did," said Evans, in his most rollicking manner. "That Sunsweet will win this afternoon by the length of a street. What a beauty, what a beauty!"

It was only by accident that Mr Frithington-Evans learned of the tragedy, and immediately burnt the telegrams he was sending and sent away his messengers. Blue and red with rage, he stamped up and down his expensive drawing-room, and visited on the head of his groom-trainer the piled up wrath which properly belonged to Educated Evans.

"We'll run the damn thing and run it down the course," he said. "Where's the horse?"

"On the course, sir," said the shivering groom, "in charge of Mr Thomson, your trainer."

Frithington-Evans seized the telephone directory and searched. There was only one number for Alexandra Park, and this he called.

"I want to talk to Mr Thomson, who is in charge of my horse," he said. "I am Mr Frithington-Evans."

"Wait a moment," said a voice.

Five minutes passed, and then somebody asked:

"Is it about Sunsweet?"

"Yes, it is." Anger made Mr Frithington-Evans incautious. "Now listen, Thomson: that horse is to run but it's not to win – do you understand – "

"Wait a moment: I think you've made a mistake," said the voice at the other end of the line. "We couldn't find your trainer. This is the senior steward speaking."

Frithy did not collapse.

"Oh – you," he said, more mildly. "I – er – meant to say that my horse isn't running."

"Your horse *is* running, Mr Frithington-Evans," said a very stern voice, "and if it can win, it will win, Mr Frithington-Evans!"

"Yes, sir," said Frithy.

He looked at his watch: it was too late to rewrite his telegrams, and his messengers had departed.

"What a beauty! What a beauty!" murmured Educated Evans.

"Hold up," said The Miller, and pushing him against the wall. "Where's your key?"

"What a beauty! What a beauty!" murmured Educated Evans, and began to sing.

"The trouble with you, Evans," said The Miller, as he dragged him up the stairs and flung him on to bed, "is that you can't carry corn. A little success drives you mad."

"What a beauty! What a beauty!" murmured Evans, and, so murmuring, fell asleep.

EDGAR WALLACE

BIG FOOT

Footprints and a dead woman bring together Superintendent Minton and the amateur sleuth Mr Cardew. Who is the man in the shrubbery? Who is the singer of the haunting Moorish tune? Why is Hannah Shaw so determined to go to Pawsy, 'a dog lonely place' she had previously detested? Death lurks in the dark and someone must solve the mystery before BIG FOOT strikes again, in a yet more fiendish manner.

BONES IN LONDON

The new Managing Director of Schemes Ltd has an elegant London office and a theatrically dressed assistant – however, Bones, as he is better known, is bored. Luckily there is a slump in the shipping market and it is not long before Joe and Fred Pole pay Bones a visit. They are totally unprepared for Bones' unnerving style of doing business, unprepared for his unique style of innocent and endearing mischief.

Edgar Wallace

Bones of the River

'Taking the little paper from the pigeon's leg, Hamilton saw it was from Sanders and marked URGENT. *Send Bones instantly to Lujamalababa… Arrest and bring to headquarters the witch doctor.*'

It is a time when the world's most powerful nations are vying for colonial honour, a time of trading steamers and tribal chiefs. In the mysterious African territories administered by Commissioner Sanders, Bones persistently manages to create his own unique style of innocent and endearing mischief.

The Daffodil Mystery

When Mr Thomas Lyne, poet, poseur and owner of Lyne's Emporium insults a cashier, Odette Rider, she resigns. Having summoned detective Jack Tarling to investigate another employee, Mr Milburgh, Lyne now changes his plans. Tarling and his Chinese companion refuse to become involved. They pay a visit to Odette's flat and in the hall Tarling meets Sam, convicted felon and protégé of Lyne. Next morning Tarling discovers a body. The hands are crossed on the breast, adorned with a handful of daffodils.

EDGAR WALLACE

THE JOKER
(USA: THE COLOSSUS)

While the millionaire Stratford Harlow is in Princetown, not only does he meet with his lawyer Mr Ellenbury but he gets his first glimpse of the beautiful Aileen Rivers, niece of the actor and convicted felon Arthur Ingle. When Aileen is involved in a car accident on the Thames Embankment, the driver is James Carlton of Scotland Yard. Later that evening Carlton gets a call. It is Aileen. She needs help.

THE SQUARE EMERALD
(USA: THE GIRL FROM SCOTLAND YARD)

'Suicide on the left,' says Chief Inspector Coldwell pleasantly, as he and Leslie Maughan stride along the Thames Embankment during a brutally cold night. A gaunt figure is sprawled across the parapet. But Coldwell soon discovers that Peter Dawlish, fresh out of prison for forgery, is not considering suicide but murder. Coldwell suspects Druze as the intended victim. Maughan disagrees. If Druze dies, she says, 'It will be because he does not love children!'

OTHER TITLES BY EDGAR WALLACE AVAILABLE DIRECT
FROM HOUSE OF STRATUS

Quantity		£	$(US)	$(CAN)	€
	THE ADMIRABLE CARFEW	6.99	12.95	19.95	13.50
	THE ANGEL OF TERROR	6.99	12.95	19.95	13.50
	THE AVENGER (USA: THE HAIRY ARM)	6.99	12.95	19.95	13.50
	BARBARA ON HER OWN	6.99	12.95	19.95	13.50
	BIG FOOT	6.99	12.95	19.95	13.50
	THE BLACK ABBOT	6.99	12.95	19.95	13.50
	BONES	6.99	12.95	19.95	13.50
	BONES IN LONDON	6.99	12.95	19.95	13.50
	BONES OF THE RIVER	6.99	12.95	19.95	13.50
	THE CLUE OF THE NEW PIN	6.99	12.95	19.95	13.50
	THE CLUE OF THE SILVER KEY	6.99	12.95	19.95	13.50
	THE CLUE OF THE TWISTED CANDLE	6.99	12.95	19.95	13.50
	THE COAT OF ARMS (USA: THE ARRANWAYS MYSTERY)	6.99	12.95	19.95	13.50
	THE COUNCIL OF JUSTICE	6.99	12.95	19.95	13.50
	THE CRIMSON CIRCLE	6.99	12.95	19.95	13.50
	THE DAFFODIL MYSTERY	6.99	12.95	19.95	13.50
	THE DARK EYES OF LONDON (USA: THE CROAKERS)	6.99	12.95	19.95	13.50
	THE DAUGHTERS OF THE NIGHT	6.99	12.95	19.95	13.50
	A DEBT DISCHARGED	6.99	12.95	19.95	13.50
	THE DEVIL MAN	6.99	12.95	19.95	13.50
	THE DOOR WITH SEVEN LOCKS	6.99	12.95	19.95	13.50
	THE DUKE IN THE SUBURBS	6.99	12.95	19.95	13.50
	THE FACE IN THE NIGHT	6.99	12.95	19.95	13.50
	THE FEATHERED SERPENT	6.99	12.95	19.95	13.50
	THE FLYING SQUAD	6.99	12.95	19.95	13.50
	THE FORGER (USA: THE CLEVER ONE)	6.99	12.95	19.95	13.50
	THE FOUR JUST MEN	6.99	12.95	19.95	13.50
	FOUR SQUARE JANE	6.99	12.95	19.95	13.50

ALL HOUSE OF STRATUS BOOKS ARE AVAILABLE FROM GOOD BOOKSHOPS
OR DIRECT FROM THE PUBLISHER:

Internet: www.houseofstratus.com including synopses and features.

Email: sales@houseofstratus.com
info@houseofstratus.com
(please quote author, title and credit card details.)

OTHER TITLES BY EDGAR WALLACE AVAILABLE DIRECT FROM HOUSE OF STRATUS

Quantity		£	$(US)	$(CAN)	€
☐	THE FOURTH PLAGUE	6.99	12.95	19.95	13.50
☐	THE FRIGHTENED LADY	6.99	12.95	19.95	13.50
☐	GOOD EVANS	6.99	12.95	19.95	13.50
☐	THE HAND OF POWER	6.99	12.95	19.95	13.50
☐	THE IRON GRIP	6.99	12.95	19.95	13.50
☐	THE JOKER (USA: THE COLOSSUS)	6.99	12.95	19.95	13.50
☐	THE JUST MEN OF CORDOVA	6.99	12.95	19.95	13.50
☐	THE KEEPERS OF THE KING'S PEACE	6.99	12.95	19.95	13.50
☐	THE LAW OF THE FOUR JUST MEN	6.99	12.95	19.95	13.50
☐	THE LONE HOUSE MYSTERY	6.99	12.95	19.95	13.50
☐	THE MAN WHO BOUGHT LONDON	6.99	12.95	19.95	13.50
☐	THE MAN WHO KNEW	6.99	12.95	19.95	13.50
☐	THE MAN WHO WAS NOBODY	6.99	12.95	19.95	13.50
☐	THE MIND OF MR J G REEDER (USA: THE MURDER BOOK OF J G REEDER)	6.99	12.95	19.95	13.50
☐	MR J G REEDER RETURNS (USA: MR REEDER RETURNS)	6.99	12.95	19.95	13.50
☐	MR JUSTICE MAXELL	6.99	12.95	19.95	13.50
☐	RED ACES	6.99	12.95	19.95	13.50
☐	ROOM 13	6.99	12.95	19.95	13.50
☐	SANDERS	6.99	12.95	19.95	13.50
☐	SANDERS OF THE RIVER	6.99	12.95	19.95	13.50
☐	THE SINISTER MAN	6.99	12.95	19.95	13.50
☐	THE SQUARE EMERALD (USA: THE GIRL FROM SCOTLAND YARD)	6.99	12.95	19.95	13.50
☐	THE THREE JUST MEN	6.99	12.95	19.95	13.50
☐	THE THREE OAK MYSTERY	6.99	12.95	19.95	13.50
☐	THE TRAITOR'S GATE	6.99	12.95	19.95	13.50
☐	WHEN THE GANGS CAME TO LONDON	6.99	12.95	19.95	13.50

Tel: Order Line
        0800 169 1780 (UK)
         800 724 1100 (USA)
        International
        +44 (0) 1845 527700 (UK)
        +01   845 463 1100 (USA)

Fax: +44 (0) 1845 527711 (UK)
        +01   845 463 0018 (USA)
        (please quote author, title and credit card details.)

Send to: House of Stratus Sales Department
         Thirsk Industrial Park
         York Road, Thirsk
         North Yorkshire, YO7 3BX
         UK

PAYMENT

Please tick currency you wish to use:

☐ £ (Sterling)   ☐ $ (US)   ☐ $ (CAN)   ☐ € (Euros)

Allow for shipping costs charged per order plus an amount per book as set out in the tables below:

CURRENCY/DESTINATION

	£(Sterling)	$(US)	$(CAN)	€ (Euros)
Cost per order				
UK	1.50	2.25	3.50	2.50
Europe	3.00	4.50	6.75	5.00
North America	3.00	3.50	5.25	5.00
Rest of World	3.00	4.50	6.75	5.00
Additional cost per book				
UK	0.50	0.75	1.15	0.85
Europe	1.00	1.50	2.25	1.70
North America	1.00	1.00	1.50	1.70
Rest of World	1.50	2.25	3.50	3.00

PLEASE SEND CHEQUE OR INTERNATIONAL MONEY ORDER
payable to: HOUSE OF STRATUS LTD or HOUSE OF STRATUS INC. or card payment as indicated

STERLING EXAMPLE

Cost of book(s):...................... Example: 3 x books at £6.99 each: £20.97

Cost of order: .... Example: £1.50 (Delivery to UK address)

Additional cost per book:............... Example: 3 x £0.50: £1.50

Order total including shipping:.......... Example: £23.97

VISA, MASTERCARD, SWITCH, AMEX:

☐ ☐

Issue number (Switch only):

☐☐☐

Start Date: **Expiry Date:**

☐☐/ ☐☐   ☐☐/ ☐☐

Signature: _____

NAME: _____

ADDRESS: _____

COUNTRY: _____

ZIP/POSTCODE: _____

Please allow 28 days for delivery. Despatch normally within 48 hours.

Prices subject to change without notice.
Please tick box if you do not wish to receive any additional information. ☐

House of Stratus publishes many other titles in this genre; please check our website (**www.houseofstratus.com**) for more details.